The Coded Papyrus

A thrilling Egyptian adventure.

Enigma in Rome

Save Caesar and face Rome's hidden challenges.

The Cursed Empress

Navigate Atlantis's secrets to break a powerful curse.

The Sun Disk

Race against time to save the Incas.

The Magic Chalice

Spooky thrills in Dracula's realm.

The Great Christmas Rescue

An adventure into Santa's realm to save Christmas.

The Druids' Secret

A magical quest to recover Excalibur and reshape history.

The Baker Street Mystery

A cryptic case to outsmart a mastermind and rescue Sir Arthur Conan Doyle.

Cover art and characters' illustrations by Draftss (https://draftss.com/)

APICEM PUBLISHING

Apicem Publishing
1309 Coffeen Avenue STE 1200
Sheridan, WY 82801, United States
www.apicempublishing.com

Published in 2024
Copyright © Coline Monsarrat , 2023
Aria & Liam ® is a trademark of Coline Monsarrat, 2022
All rights reserved.

ISBN (paperback): 978-1-959814-20-7
ISBN (ebook): 978-1-959814-21-4

ARIA & LIAM

The History Detectives

The Baker Street Mystery

Coline
Monsarrat

APICEM PUBLISHING

Hey fellow adventurers, meet Liam! He is my best friend and partner in crime! He's a 13-year-old kid from Sommetville who can code up a storm and kick a soccer ball like a pro. When we're not in class, you can usually find him doing one of those things. Unless, of course, I've got some wild idea to drag us into trouble - and let's be honest, I usually do!

One time, I even dragged us straight into a 3,000-year-old kingdom. Can you believe it? At first, Liam wasn't exactly thrilled, especially when I started rambling on about history like a super-enthusiastic professor. Hey, I could talk about historical stuff for hours – it's my thing! But guess what? My nerdy history knowledge actually came in handy and saved our bacon more than a few times. And let's not forget Liam's mad archery skills – we'd be royally stuck without them!

Now we're like heroes of the past, with people from all over calling on us to save the day. It's pretty crazy, and even though Liam freaks out every time we get transported to a different time period, he secretly loves our adventures. Just don't tell him I said that, or he'll never let me live it down!

Hey there, fellow adventurers! Let me introduce you to my partner-in-crime, Aria! She's not your average 13-year-old - this girl has a serious obsession with history. Seriously, don't even try to challenge her, or she'll beat you every time. That's why I call her the walking encyclopedia!

Aria's motto is to live life to the fullest, even if it means breaking a few rules (which happens a lot when I'm around). But her curiosity is what led us on an epic adventure through the Kingdom of Ramesses II, a place that's older than my grandpa's grandpa's grandpa. At first, I wasn't too thrilled, but I have to admit, it's kind of grown on me (don't tell Aria, though!).

And get this, not only do we travel through time, but I also get to enjoy beating Aria in sports! I mean, who doesn't love the feeling of outsmarting your best friend?

So buckle up, adventurers, because Aria and I are about to take you on a wild ride through history!

CONTENTS

The Baker Street Mystery

Let the adventure begin

THE CHARACTERS

ARIA

LIAM

SIR ARTHUR
CONAN DOYLE

MARY LOUISE
DOYLE

LOUISA DOYLE

JAMES

LORD
MONTGOMERY

DR. WATSON

BARONESS
ORCZY

CHAPTER I
221B BAKER STREET

I n the heart of Sherlock Holmes' study at 221b Baker Street, Aria and Liam stand before a framed front page of the *Daily News* from 1902 announcing the mysterious disappearance of its author, Sir Arthur Conan Doyle.

Aria heaves a heavy sigh as she reads the inscription below, providing details of the enigma that occurred over a century ago. "What a tragedy! Can you imagine? Disappearing like this without a trace!" She makes her way over to a cluttered desk filled with tools that the fictional detective relies on to solve his cases.

"That's sad," Liam says, "but after all, this man was just an author."

Liam shifts his posture, aware of Aria's eyes fixed

on him. "Just an author? He's the one behind Sherlock Holmes!"

"Sure, I like Sherlock Holmes, but it's not like he changed the world! Not like us," he says, winking at her.

Aria cannot hold back a smile as she shakes her head before spotting an old magnifying glass in the middle of the desk. She sneaks a glance around to locate their history teacher, Mrs. Thompson, before smirking at the small sign that reads, "Do not touch."

Liam's eyebrows shoot up as he realizes what his best friend is plotting. During their two-day school trip to London, Aria managed to get them into so much trouble that they were on the brink of receiving detention every day after school for the rest of the year. Avoiding any further mishaps is now essential.

"Aria, don't even think about it," Liam warns, his eyes wide with concern.

Aria tilts her head, her lips curving into a slight pout. "Oh, come on, Liam. Don't be such a wimp! It's Sherlock Holmes' magnifying glass!"

Liam rolls his eyes. "Stop kidding yourself! You know Sherlock Holmes isn't real; he never owned this!" he retorts, prompting a laugh from her.

"True, but it's a nineteenth-century artifact! And that, my dear Liam is worth investigating!" she declares, grabbing the handle. Her curious eyes sparkle as she examines the object, moving it from side to side. Liam leans in, his initial reluctance giving way to intrigue.

"Aria! Liam! What are you two up to again?" Mrs. Thompson's voice booms, causing all the students to startle. Before Aria can put down the object, their teacher stands behind them, impressive and stern.

"Uh..." Liam mumbles, his face pinched with anxiety.

Aria gently places the magnifying glass back on the desk and turns to Mrs. Thompson with a grin that reaches her ears. "I'm sorry, Mrs. Thompson. You'll surely understand once we explain," she says boldly, making Liam frown.

Mrs. Thompson's face wrinkles even more. "I doubt that, but go on, Aria."

Aria stands tall, her smile firm. "Liam was challenging the authenticity of this piece," she begins, making Liam frown even more. "He dared to say it's from the twentieth century. Can you believe it?" she asks with a gasp. She picks up the magnifying glass again and presents it to Mrs. Thompson, whose stern look is slowly fading. "See the design on the handle?" she points out. "It's clearly the late nineteenth century, not the twentieth! I just couldn't let Liam spread such inaccuracies!" she exclaims with conviction.

Liam's face contorts. He is stunned as Mrs. Thompson's features soften while she looks at them both. Standing up straight, Liam holds his breath while he awaits their punishment.

Their history teacher straightens her formal gray suit. "Well, Aria," she says, offering the girl a smile. "Your enthusiasm for history is certainly impressive, but that doesn't permit you to put your hands on museum items!" Her face suddenly turns serious.

"I'm sorry, Mrs. Thompson," Aria apologizes in a subdued tone.

Mrs. Thompson glares at them through her rectangular glasses. Liam remains frozen, a taut look on his face, while Aria preserves her beaming smile. "I'm keeping an eye on you two," she says sternly, raising a finger at them. "You've caused enough problems since we got here to London already; another act of insubordination will land you in detention for the rest of the semester!" She pauses, making sure they take her warning seriously. "Do you understand?"

"Yes," Liam mumbles, his expression blank.

"We give you our word!" Aria exclaims.

Mrs. Thompson quickly makes her way to the next room, and the students silently observing the scene resume their conversations. Liam's face shifts to an expression of disbelief as he turns to Aria. "We? You were the one who wanted to touch it!" he reproaches.

Aria rolls her eyes. "You were just as eager to

look at it," she retorts casually. "Besides, I got us out of trouble. Did you see how convincingly I acted?"

Liam looks at her, his annoyance fading into a smile as he stays silent.

The museum guide's voice cuts through. "Everyone! Let's proceed to the laboratory room where Sherlock Holmes analyzed his evidence! The world's first forensic lab!" he announces with gusto.

Aria hurries along with the crowd toward the lab, rhythmically tapping her legs to resist rushing ahead.

"Aria!" Liam calls, weaving through to her side. "Wait up!"

Aria halts suddenly in the hallway, captivated by a doorway separating the office and lab. Other students hurry past her, eager to enter the lab, leaving her and Liam alone in the corridor of the elegant Georgian townhouse.

She inches toward the wooden door, reading the sign:

Renovation in progress — Do Not Enter.

"Don't even think about it," Liam interjects from behind, startling her. "I refuse to spend the year in detention because you can't control your curiosity!" he cautions, but his words are lost on her.

She spins around. "Oh, come on, Liam! Aren't

you curious about what's behind it?" she pleads, her curiosity boiling.

"The last thing I want is to explain to my mom why I'm in detention all year," he responds, his eyes wide.

Aria winces, understanding Liam's dilemma. She knows his mother's strict stance all too well—strictness on a level that surpasses school detention. In contrast, Aria's father is the opposite; he can never bring himself to punish her and instead gives in too quickly.

She glances around. "Come on, Liam, they're so engrossed they won't even notice we're gone!" Before her best friend can argue, she opens the door and enters the faintly lit room.

She inhales the smell of new paint as she looks around. The wallpaper looks worn in a few places, and sheets cover the furniture.

"Aria! Come back!" Liam calls, hastening to retrieve her.

But before he can reach her, a window opens, and a gust of wind slams the door closed behind him. Aria and Liam both jump as the walls shake from the force. The clanging sound from outside startles them once again. Aria looks at Liam, who appears to be spooked, his breaths coming in short bursts. "Admit it. You were scared we'd stumbled into some wild adventure!" she teases, followed by a laugh.

Liam steadies himself and wipes his forehead. "You're mistaken, my dear Aria! I was just bracing myself for the next twist—"

Suddenly, the chandelier overhead rattles and a clock chimes. A small twister begins to swirl around them, trapping them in the room as objects shift and move erratically.

A painting representing a man falls to the ground near Aria. With the earthquake intensifying beneath them, the two desperately search for an exit. Liam takes Aria's hand and pulls her out of the tornado toward the door. He wraps his fingers around the doorknob and pulls it open swiftly. They quickly step out onto the landing, and Liam forcefully shuts the door behind them, muffling all sounds of chaos from within.

They stand silently, catching their breath as they lean against the door. "Was that an earthquake?" Aria finally exhales, her breath still shaky and uneven.

"An earthquake? In London?" Liam responds, his voice laced with disbelief. He moves toward the closed lab door and says, "We should meet the others. Hopefully, they will have an answer to what happened! We must not have been the only ones to feel it." He sweeps away the sweat on his forehead with his hand, his breath still coming in gasps.

"I sure have a way of spicing up your life!" she says with a chuckle, her voice trailing off as she takes in the view. She squints as she sees the small lamps attached to the walls. She could swear flames were emerging from the brass fixtures, casting a soft glow across the staircase. How can it be possible?

Liam rolls his eyes. "Don't get ahead of yourself—"

"I shall fetch her, my lady." A deep, authoritative female voice carries toward them, making them freeze on the spot. Their faces turn to shock as a woman, wearing an old-fashioned black dress and white apron, appears from the bottom of the stairwell.

CHAPTER 2
NOT THE SAME ERA

L iam covers his mouth to silence his heavy panting. As the woman nears the bend in the stairs, Aria grabs Liam's arm and pulls him back into the room they had sprinted away from a few moments before. She shuts the door and spins to face him. They remain still, eyes fixed on each other. Aria finally glances around, her eyes growing bigger and bigger as she surveys the room.

Gone are the drapes and the scent of paint. The room is crowded with furniture and decorations, the air thick with a musty scent. Dark green chairs stand out against the dark wooden floors, while a piano sits in the corner. Compared to the previous room they entered, this one seems smaller due to the abundance of paintings framed in ornate gold and various trinkets and rugs scattered around.

Seeing the shock in his best friend's eyes, Liam turns around and gasps in surprise. "What's happening?" he stammers, his voice laced with fear.

"It looks like your wish for an adventure wasn't so far off, Liam!" Aria quips.

"No, this can't be right. Maybe we entered a different room by mistake!" he suggests, his knees nearly buckling.

Aria faces him squarely. "Which room, Liam? And keep your voice down. That woman might hear us."

The image of the old woman flashes through Liam's mind. "There has to be an explanation. Maybe the museum has actors to enhance the experience!" he rationalizes.

Ignoring Liam's speculations, Aria focuses on the wallpaper. This pattern stands out from the rest of the museum's decorations. The white flowers and sea-green leaves look stunning against the emerald background, nothing like the Georgian style of the museum's townhouse.

"We need to get back to the others," Liam insists, his voice shaking.

"How do you suppose we do that?" Aria challenges, a crease forming on her forehead.

"We just walk back the same way we came," Liam replies, a hint of exasperation in his voice.

Aria shakes her head. "If you haven't noticed, we might have just traveled through time," she says as she gestures to their surroundings.

"This room looks the same as all the ones we have seen! You're letting your imagination get the better of you once more," Liam counters.

Aria strides to the wall, unshakeable. "You are the one refusing to see the obvious once more! Look closer at the wallpaper. This is Victorian. The Sherlock Holmes Museum is Georgian," she insists.

Liam's expression morphs into one of comical disbelief. As he opens his mouth to respond, a sound resembling a horse's whinny interrupts him. After a quick silence, he mutters, "Maybe it's just a show!" He glances around the room frantically before turning toward the wall, his hands patting the area near the door.

"What are you doing?" Aria strides over to him in exasperation.

"I'm looking for the light switch! It's too dark!" he exclaims, a note of frustration in his voice.

"You won't find one—there's no electricity in

this era, Liam! Didn't you see the gas lamp in the corridor?"

He exhales deeply and faces her. "Instead of dreaming up adventures, let's return with the others. Mrs. Thompson will have our heads if we don't." Suddenly, he winces, a foul odor assaulting his senses.

"What's wrong now?" Aria asks, her hands folded in front of her waist as she stares at him.

"Don't you smell that? It's like chemicals," he says, shaking his head as his eyes water.

Aria sniffs the air, and her nose wrinkles. "You're right. It smells like..." She pauses, her expression brightening up. "Liam! This is additional proof we're in the past!" she exclaims.

"Sh! Be quiet! Do you want this woman to catch us and inform Mrs. Thompson?" he hisses.

Aria lifts her eyebrows in mock surprise. "That would be difficult! But you're right. We should be quiet since we don't know where we are," she whispers. Her eyes sparkle as she connects the dots. "This wallpaper—it's from the past. I watched a documentary that mentioned that wallpapers in Victorian homes contained harmful substances, like the green pigment they often used back then. It was arsenic-based and trendy during the nineteenth century."

Liam steps away from the wallpaper, his face a mask of shock. "Are you serious? And you let me touch that?" he exclaims, his voice rising.

"I thought you didn't believe we had traveled through time, Liam!"

Before Liam can retort, footsteps and voices outside the room spike their anxiety. Aria scans the room for a hiding spot. "There! Behind that screen." She points to a folding screen near the fireplace and window. She dashes over to it, urging Liam to join her. They swiftly hide behind the partition before the door swings open.

Aria spies through a slim gap between the panels while Liam stays silently behind, his heart pounding in his chest.

A woman in her early forties enters the room. Her brown locks are styled in delicate waves, and she carries herself with poise and confidence. Her long dress drapes elegantly around her waist, cascading to the floor like a waterfall. She stands tall with a perfect posture. Her high-necked blouse adorned with subtle ruffles makes her look taller. The other woman from the stairwell follows closely behind, her expression serious.

"Lady Doyle, I assure you I will address Mary Louise's behavior," the latter says. Aria frowns before biting her lip as she hears the name.

Lady Doyle strides to a cabinet and withdraws a small envelope.

"I trust you will, Nurse Penny. I just can't fathom what's gotten into her. She's never been this unruly," she says with a sigh, her voice laced with concern.

"If the master were less lenient with his..." The nurse's lips purse in distaste before she proceeds, "paranormal endeavors, Miss Mary Louise might be less... imaginative," she concludes, her lips curling into a wry smile.

Lady Doyle's smirk reveals her amusement at Nurse Penny's pointed observation. "I'm afraid my husband is uninclined to abandon his spiritualist pursuits any time soon, Nurse Penny. You'd best acclimate to it," she responds, eliciting an eye roll from the nurse. Handing her the envelope, she instructs, "Please ensure this is sent promptly. Mr. Clifford is preoccupied with pressing matters and cannot attend to them. And don't fret over Miss Mary Louise; confinement to her room should suffice to keep her in check." With that, Lady Doyle moves towards the corridor.

"Certainly, my lady. Shall I arrange for a meal to be sent to Miss Mary Louise?" Nurse Penny inquires.

Pausing, Lady Doyle turns back with a contemplative look. "Yes, do that. Have her remain in the nursery for the day, and perhaps we might ease her punishment this evening. Our return to Undershaw might restore her usual demeanor." She's interrupted by a fit of coughing, her complexion fading as the bout intensifies. Nurse Penny jumps to her aid, patting her back gently.

Lady Doyle finally regains her composure. "Thank you, Nurse Penny. I'll retire to my chamber for a rest," she says before exiting the room, the nurse in tow.

Once the door closes, Aria eyes Liam intently, noticing his pale face. His eyes look around like a lost puppy before settling on the window. His hand shakes as he gestures outside. "A-Aria," he barely manages to get out.

She gazes out at the cobblestone street bustling with activity. Despite the torrential rain, people are elegantly clothed and hurrying between horse-drawn carriages and omnibuses. This is definitely different from the London they have seen.

CHAPTER 3
MARY LOUISE DOYLE

Aria steps closer to the window, her face alight with wonder as she observes the lively street below. The clatter of horses' hooves mixes with the honking of early automobiles as people cross the road in organized chaos. Women in lavish dresses carry umbrellas despite the lack of sun, while men wear perfectly fitted three-piece suits, signaling wealth with their watch chains and the rhythmic tap of canes on the cobblestones.

"This is incredible!" Aria breathes, her face beaming with excitement.

Liam rubs his eyes, disbelieving. "This is crazy! Where are we?" He blinks rapidly, trying to make sense of the scene.

"Based on what we're seeing, I'd say the turn of

the twentieth century," Aria says, her gaze darting around to gather clues from the street. She points to a horse-drawn omnibus, a late Victorian-era vehicle, the sides of which indicate 'Camden' as its destination. "We're definitely in London!"

The concept of a horse-driven bus makes Liam's head spin as he steps closer to the window. A draft of cool air gives him a shiver. Aria grasps Liam's arm, her eyes widening. "Doyle! We must be around the 1900s!" she exclaims.

Liam's frown deepens. "What do you mean?"

"Don't you see? We must be here to save Sir Arthur Conan Doyle!" Aria prompts incredulously.

Liam's face turns from confusion to astonishment. "You mean find him?"

"Yes, my dear Liam! We are at it again! We need to make sure we are here for that!" She grabs his arm, shaking him from his stupor before rushing into the center of the living room. Her face contorts as her knee hits a footrest. Flashes of red spread on her face as she bites her fist to refrain from screaming in pain. Liam stays motionless, trying to put all the events together. Aria finally regains her composure, snapping her fingers in his direction. "Liam! Stop staring and come help!"

Liam braces himself to join her. Aria has been

right enough for today. There is no way he will give her another opportunity to tease him about what she calls his "acclimation period." He must face the truth: They're embroiled in another quest, and solving it is the only way to return home. He knows the rule all too well by now.

"Do you think he has already disappeared?" Liam asks her as he meets her next to the desk where Lady Doyle stood not long ago.

Aria stops rifling through the desk's compartments to think. "Nope!" she responds confidently. "Remember what the nurse said—it doesn't seem like he's gone yet! Can you imagine? We will be able to save one of the best authors in the world!" she exclaims so enthusiastically that Liam wonders if she realizes the task ahead. Aria pauses, her gaze landing on the book-filled shelves. She turns to Liam, her expression grave.

"What is it?" Liam asks, his jaw set tight.

"Do you remember when Conan Doyle killed off Sherlock Holmes and how his fans were outraged?" Aria prompts. Liam winces, his attention focused on her. "The public backlash was immense; people even canceled subscriptions to the magazine that published the stories. Doyle received so many angry letters from fans!"

"All that because he killed a fictional character?"

Aria sights in disbelief. "It is not just any fictional character, my dear Liam! It is Sherlock Holmes! People even thought he was real!"

"Okay… If you say so… But do you really think someone would commit a kidnapping for something like this?"

"I don't know, some people are nuts."

"Maybe he just left on his own; who knows?"

"But if it's the case, why are we here? And how could no one have seen him again?"

Liam begins to feel nervous. "Do you think he was killed?" he dares to ask.

Aria strides forward, her expression somber. "No one ever found out what happened to him. And you know the worst part? People said only someone as brilliant as Sherlock Holmes could have solved the mystery."

MARY LOUISE LIES on her bed, her gaze transfixed on the ceiling as she replays her morning argument with her parents. She rises abruptly and strides to her desk. Opening a drawer, she takes out a leather-bound notebook secured with a strap. After loosening the knot, she flips to an empty page. Drawing out a fountain pen, Mary Louise dips the nib into some ink and scribbles away.

Dear Journal,

I'm in my room, where Mama just punished me severely. They'll never understand, and now I'm fighting back tears. I tried warning them about what I knew, but they wouldn't listen! I thought Papa might believe me since he is the one who taught me to look for signs from the universe. But for some reason, he didn't this time. They think I'm overreacting because we're in London for the season, and I'm hitting my teenage years.

When I received the threatening letter yesterday, I thought my heart would stop. I can't stop fretting over the disaster that might befall Papa if the message is correct. When I showed my parents the letter, they dismissed it as if I had written it to get attention. Can you believe it? Now, they want to send me *back to Undershaw with Arthur. Speaking of Arthur, it's a relief he's not here to see these dreadful things unfold—he's too little. Nanny Penny insists I shouldn't have come to London. She says it's filling my head with nonsense. You should've seen her reaction when Papa mentioned the spirit world a few days ago—she was gripping her cross as if my father was a demon. She disagrees with his spiritual views and does everything she can to stop me from following his path. But for now, I need assistance from a higher power more than ever. I've been praying since yesterday, yet nothing has happened. I can't fight alone.*

Mary Louise looks away from her notebook when she hears the creaking sound of somebody walking in the hall. She pauses to listen carefully. After moments of stillness, she picks up the pen and resumes writing.

Mama's been coughing a lot more these days. They consulted a new doctor but kept me in the dark about what he said. They think I'm too young to understand such matters, but they're mistaken. I'm already thirteen! When will they finally take me seriously?

Tears cloud her vision, one smudging the words on the page. A sudden thump startles her. Hastily, she slams her diary shut and stashes it away. She quickly returns to her bed and grabs a book from her nightstand. Wiping the tear that escaped her eyes, she takes a deep breath and tries to look as if she's engrossed in what she's reading.

CHAPTER 4
THE ALARMING NOTE

Aria and Liam lock eyes without a word. Is their mission to save one of the greatest authors from an untimely death? Liam nervously wipes his face. The last time they had to save somebody from a murder attempt, he almost got devoured by a lion.

"We need to find out who brought us here!" Aria says abruptly, snapping Liam back to reality. She strides to the door, her hand poised on the knob.

"Hold on!" Liam says, rushing to her side. "What's our plan? We can't risk being seen by someone who did not call for us."

Aria bites her lip. "You're right, but standing here won't help either! What if someone comes?

Look at how we are dressed compared to all of them!"

Liam glances down at his outfit and tilts his head quizzically. "What's wrong with it? I look awesome!"

"That may be true for our time, but you stick out like a sore thumb here!"

"Fine, but to go where? We're not even sure we're here to save him! Your theory might be a mix of historical facts," he retorts, prompting a blush to creep across Aria's cheeks.

"If you've got a better idea, I'm all ears."

Liam exhales deeply. "Alright, you win. Just promise me you won't take any reckless risks—"

"I won't, Liam. We'll exit the house and figure it out from there."

"Go out into the street? How do you suppose we'll manage that? And have you seen the rain?"

Aria dismisses his concerns and pushes down the handle, cracking the door open just enough to peek into the hallway.

"Aria!" Liam whispers with frustration.

She opens the door slowly, the wood creaking under its strain. Aria grits her teeth, her pulse racing. Cautiously, she steps onto the opulent red carpet, avoiding the squeaky floorboards. She nods in Liam's direction, gesturing for him to come.

He swallows loudly as he moves cautiously and methodically outside, trying his best not to shake. As Liam prepares to take another step, raised voices echo up from below. The wooden steps creak under someone's weight.

He immediately stops mid-step, one leg still in the air.

"It must be in the cabinet upstairs," a man's voice says, his steps drawing nearer.

Aria locks eyes with Liam, seeing his breath fogging the cold air. Immediately, she grabs hold of his arm and tugs him up the stairway. Every tread gives a screeching creak of complaint.

"Mary Louise?" the man's voice calls, propelling the two with greater urgency. As they climb the final step, they see a group of closed doors. Their hearts are pounding in their chests, and they struggle to catch their breath. Without hesitation, Liam reaches for the closest one and rushes inside, quickly followed by Aria.

Liam jumps back with a startled cry, and Aria gasps as they discover a young girl sitting on a bed.

Mary Louise's gaze appears to be filled with mixed feelings as she stands up. Her curly brown hair cascades over her shoulders, and the light fabric of her long dress falls past her sparkling white boots.

Her dress's high collar and lace-trimmed ruffles make a bold contrast to her bare arms.

The sound of footsteps outside fades away until there is only silence. Aria and Liam remain motionless, not daring to move a muscle. Mary Louise steps closer. "Who are you?" Fear and curiosity mix in her tone.

"Who are we?" Liam's voice quivers. "Who are *you*?"

Aria clears her throat. "Remember, we're the outsiders here, Liam."

Liam's breathing becomes more labored, his brow furrowing in distress. Finally, Aria relaxes and takes a step forward.

"This is Liam, and I'm Aria. We are..." She stops to think for a moment before finishing her thought, "adventurers," she says with a comforting smile.

Mary Louise's face lights up with joy as she exclaims, "It worked!" She quickly covers her mouth in surprise, and a few tears of relief well up in her eyes. Looking to the sky with one hand raised in prayer, she mutters, "Thank you."

Liam's tension drops a bit as he joins Aria.

"Are you the one who asked for our help?" Aria asks.

"I guess the answer is yes. When I asked for assistance, I had no idea they would send people. Are you some kind of magician?"

Liam chuckles nervously. "Magician? Us? You will have to put your hopes away because—"

"He wants to say that we do not have magic or any powers. We are from the future!" Aria interjects, her chest heaving.

A wave of disappointment washes over Mary Louise. "The future? But how can you possibly help us?"

Aria grunts in frustration. "We're not sure yet. We usually go with the flow..."

Mary Louise scrunches her eyebrows in confusion.

"Maybe you can tell us why you need our help before judging our abilities," Liam intervenes.

Mary Louise stares at them, her voice shaking with emotion. "My dad is in trouble," she says, attempting to control her tears.

"Do you mean Sir Arthur Conan Doyle?" Aria asks.

Mary Louise nods with a proud but anxious smile. "Yes, the most famous author in the world."

Liam winces at this level of confidence. "Sure,

he is famous. But not as famous as the fictional character he created."

Liam startles at Mary Louise's sudden gasp and watches as she scurries to the bookshelf. She digs through the books until her fingers find one, quickly flipping through its pages. She stops and presents it open to him and Aria. They gasp in shock as they see the drawing of themselves with their beloved pet Pingo.

"That's you! You're the heroes from Atlantis." Mary Louise exclaims, her excitement stark against the pair's astonishment.

"Can you believe this, Aria? We've made a name for ourselves!" Liam smiles widely, his chest puffing.

Aria gives him a mockingly disbelieving look. "Just make sure your head doesn't get too big. Otherwise, it won't fit through door frames! Might become complicated when we travel."

"Are you sure? Doors we find in history are quite big!" he says jokingly, drawing a playful smirk from Aria.

Aria gazes intently at Mary Louise. "What year is it?"

"We are in 1902. Why?"

Aria's lips press together, the weight of bearing

bad news again hanging on her. She pushes aside this thought to concentrate on the task at hand.

"What makes you think your father is in danger?"

Mary Louise strides silently to the desk and unlocks the top drawer with a key draped around her neck. She cautiously retrieves a letter and passes it to Aria.

"I received this letter yesterday. I tried warning my parents, but they won't listen. I need your help more than ever!"

Aria opens the note. The message, written in an elegant cursive script, warns,

Beware, for your father's time
on this earth is threatened.
Evil souls seek his silence.

Aria and Liam's faces flash with worry. Given the date, the creator of Sherlock Holmes only has a few moments to live. The sound of footsteps coming up the stairs brings them back to the present moment. Mary Louise acts swiftly, pushing them both towards a large wardrobe.

"Quick, hide in here! It's likely Nanny Penny—she mustn't see you!"

Aria slides into the armoire between the voluptuous dresses while Liam takes his place on the other side. Once they are snugly within, Mary Louise quietly closes the doors before them as her Nanny enters the room.

CHAPTER 5
NANNY PENNY

"Nanny Penny!" Mary Louise exclaims in a high-pitched voice as she grabs the book she had dropped on her desk before.

Nurse Penny watches her intently as she enters, scrutinizing the area.

"Is everything alright?" Mary Louise inquires, stepping towards her Nanny to distract her from the wardrobe.

Nurse Penny leans down to look at the young girl more closely. "I came to check on you. It sounded like other voices were coming from here."

Mary Louise's heart starts racing, making her palms dampen. She walks toward her bookshelf and places back the book.

"No, Nanny Penny. Everything's fine, I was…" her voice quakes. "I was just reading aloud. That's what you heard!" she says, spinning around with a forced grin.

"I thought I heard multiple voices," Nurse Penny insists, pacing the room. Aria and Liam hold their breath as the footsteps near the wardrobe.

"Perhaps it's a ghost!" Mary Louise exclaims, her eyes sparkling.

Her Nanny whirls around, her eyes wide. "I hope you don't start fancying ghost tales like your father, dear," she chides, her brows knitting together. "Ghosts aren't real, and it would be wise to choose your books more carefully. You're letting your imagination run wild, and it's caused quite a stir with your parents."

"But I'm telling the truth!"

"Enough of that now! I came to let you know I have an errand to run for your mother. Spend this time reading something more beneficial." She takes a small book from her dress pocket and offers it to Mary Louise. The girl's expression falls as she reads the title. *Principles of Politeness, and of Knowing the World* by Lord Chesterfield. She inwardly groans. Another book preaching a woman's 'proper' role. "My friend Mary recommended it. Young Lady Victoria found it quite enlightening, and you'd do well to follow her lead, Miss Mary Louise!" she states, lifting a finger.

Mary Louise bites back a grimace. She and Victoria often cross paths at society events, and she is everything Mary Louise dreads becoming—a proper Victorian young lady. Her Nanny holds Victoria as an example, wishing Mary Louise would imitate her and abandon her independent ways. But with an unconventional father like hers, she has managed to escape such expectations.

One of Mary Louise's greatest amusements is to tease her Nanny. Still, timing is everything, and the moment is pressing. She lifts her gaze from the book and beams her most charming smile.

"Thank you, Nanny! I'll start on it right away," she says, clutching the book to her heart.

Nurse Penny gives a start, her eyebrows arching. "Well, that's a pleasant surprise," she responds warily. "I shall leave you to it then." She holds Mary Louise's gaze a moment longer before reluctantly exiting the room.

With relief, Mary Louise tosses the book onto her bed and hurries to the wardrobe just as Aria emerges, reddish and sweating. "It's like an oven in there!" she gasps, followed by Liam, equally flushed.

"An oven?" Mary Louise repeats, perplexed.

"Picture a hot volcano," Liam explains, his ability to describe modern technology becoming better with every adventure. "Anyway, you deserve an award for that performance!" he grins, prompting Mary Louise to perform an exaggerated curtsy, her hands lifting the sides of her dress.

"You're brave. Putting up with such a strict nanny must be difficult!" Aria says, fear in her eyes.

"She's as tough as a hedgehog," Mary Louise jokes. Then she clarifies for the puzzled pair, "She's quite challenging."

Aria shifts restlessly. "Now, we must find who sent you this note. We have no time to waste! Was there any clue on the envelope?"

"No, but you can look for yourself," she says as she grabs it. Aria turns the envelope to see all its facets. Except for a small blue stain that looks like a brush, the plain envelope has only the girl's name written on it.

Mary Louise's face tightens. "What happened to my father? I mean, in the future," she asks, her voice shaking.

Aria and Liam freeze, tension filling the room. "Uh, we don't know, right, Liam?"

Liam nods, avoiding Mary Louise's eyes.

"There's no point worrying over the future!" Aria insists, gripping Mary Louise's shoulder. "We're here to help your father, aren't we, Liam?" she says as she glances at him.

Liam nods, his mouth set in a thin line. Under

Aria's insistent look, he murmurs, "Absolutely," before switching subjects. "But we should change first. We can't go out looking like this."

Aria releases Mary Louise and beams. "Liam, you're adapting quite well! I'm impressed. Your adaptation period is becoming—"

"Can we focus, Aria? We're on a tight schedule with an imminent threat!" he interjects, his face taut with urgency.

"You're right," Aria says, turning to Mary Louise. "Do you have anything we can wear?" Mary Louise hesitates, then strides to the wardrobe. She presents Aria with a vibrant red dress with long sleeves and a high neck. It's tight at the top, puffy at the bottom, and goes down to her mid-calf. The embroidery near the waist gives a well-received elegant touch. Aria's face brightens when she sees the beautiful yet comfortable attire. One of her least favorite parts about visiting the past is wearing clothing that restricts her movements. Mary Louise picks up a pair of black lace-up boots. She waves her arm toward a folding screen in one corner of the room, "You can get changed there."

Aria quickly walks away, sneaking looks at the excited Liam. He can barely contain his happiness as he gets to wear clothes just like his favorite movie characters. Mary Louise watches him, her face changing from serious to joyful as she gets an idea. "Hold on, I think my brother left some clothes here," she says, heading to a wardrobe on the opposite side of the bedroom. She scours through the cabinet and brings a tailored brown tweed outfit with shorts. She adds a white shirt with a pointed collar, long socks, and black lace-up boots to the pile that is slowly toppling in Liam's arms.

Aria emerges from behind the screen with a striking twirl, smiling broadly. "This dress is awesome!"

Mary Louise claps her hands. "You look perfect for our time!"

Liam nods. "You actually do, but I will look even better!" he exclaims as he rushes behind the screen.

"I must say, I was expecting something much more constraining," Aria remarks.

"We are too young for the more glamorous yet very uncomfortable dress." Mary Louise grins. "They always look so beautiful, but you can barely breathe!" Aria nods as they both chuckle.

Liam calls them out from behind the privacy screen, a mix of surprise and despair in his voice. "Did you say your brother is a bit younger? How old is he?"

NANNY PENNY

"Ten," Mary Louise responds, a wry smile on her lips.

"TEN?" Liam's voice escalates in disbelief.

"He's quite tall for his age, though!" Mary Louise reassures him.

Aria chuckles. "Come out, Liam. We must see this!"

"No way, I'm packed in it like a sardine!"

"Let us be the judges of that," Aria pleads, half-mocking. "Or is this your way of chickening out?"

He walks out, looking annoyed. Aria tries to hold in her giggles when she sees him. His jacket looks too small for his broad shoulders, and his shirt is so tight that the buttons might pop off. The pants are too short, like breeches, turning his long socks into a necessity rather than a choice. Liam sways as the shiny black boots pinch his toes.

"I can't be seen like this!" he says, face flushed as the girls continue to laugh.

"You look… dashing, my dear Liam!" Aria manages between giggles.

Liam wraps his arms across his chest defensively. "Could you not laugh? It's hardly funny!" His plea is punctuated by a tearing sound as a seam gives way.

Aria's laughter grows louder, but it halts abruptly at the sound of something hitting the window.

The trio freezes.

CHAPTER 6
THE MYSTERIOUS RING

Mary Louise shakes off her daze and hurries to the window. She barely gets there when tiny stones hit the glass. She shuts her eyes tight, opens them, and unhooks the window's latch.

"You're nuts!" Liam yells, racing to her side as she swings open the window sashes. She leans out, her face alight with excitement.

Liam grabs her arm to pull her back inside. "Are you trying to get hurt?" he asks with alarm.

Aria and Liam jolt backward as a young boy's head pops through the window. "Hi, mate!" he greets, pressing his palms against the window's frame and swinging his legs inside. Aria and Liam stare, speechless at the boy. An overly used black cap covers his auburn locks. His oversized wool coat, pale shirt, loose trousers, and untied necktie give him the look of a rebel. A loud thud fills the room as his heavy boots step inside.

Mary Louise greets him before turning to Aria and Liam. "Let me introduce you to James Evans, my best friend in London!"

"Nice to meet you all!" James says, offering his hand.

Aria is the first to shake it in silence as she observes him in confusion. "The pleasure's all ours!" Liam follows with a firm handshake.

They scrutinize the boy, clearly not dressed with the same sophistication as the high society. "Are you also from this neighborhood?" Aria questions.

"Me?" James points to himself, surprised by the assumption. "No, no! I am milk delivery. I do my round in this neighborhood every day."

"That's how we met," Mary Louise clarifies.

Liam frowns, leaning on Aria. "Milk delivery? Is that even a thing?"

Aria chuckles. At least their trips to the past teach her best friend about the many things they do not have to do in their time.

James looks at Mary Louise. "Is he trustworthy?"

"Yes, he's here to help. He's from..." She pauses, realizing she barely knows him.

"Sommetville!" Aria chimes in eagerly before looking serious. "We've got some questions for you," she adds.

"Hold on!" Liam cuts in, digging out his ever-ready phone. Mary Louise and James frown at the weird object. "No time to explain!" Liam adds as he sees their puzzled expressions.

Aria raises an eyebrow. "What are you doing?"

"Taking notes, like any good detective."

Aria rolls her eyes. "Haven't you noticed? There's no power here. What'll you do when your phone battery dies?"

"So, what do you propose? Rely on your memory?" Liam counters with a smirk.

Aria grins. "We could write things down on paper, like in the old days. It wouldn't hurt you to try some traditional methods, Liam!"

James leans into Mary Louise. "You've got some quirky friends!" he whispers, a grin teasing his lips, prompting a giggle from her.

"So, James, what were you doing yesterday morning?" Aria asks, raising her head high.

James straightens under Aria's commanding tone. "Why do you ask me that?"

Aria's intense gaze doesn't waver. "We need to know where you were when the note Mary Louise received was delivered."

James shifts from one foot to the other uncomfortably. As Aria keeps staring at him, he finally blurts, "You don't suspect me of wrongdoing, do you?"

Aria straightens, clearing her throat. "We can't rule anything out until we investigate."

"But he's my friend," Mary Louise says, moving to stand with James.

"And why would I do anything to harm Sir Doyle?" James asks, a hint of defiance in his voice.

"Don't worry," Liam reassures him with a grin. "Aria's just playing the hard-nosed detective. Right, Aria?" He waves his hand in front of her face. "Snap out of it. We've got a puzzle to solve. Watch out, or I'll start thinking you're the one who needs an adaptation period," he teases.

Aria shakes her head, turning back to Liam. "I wouldn't dream of giving you the satisfaction. I was just thinking about the case ahead. Sorry, James, but everyone's a suspect in a good investigation."

"Even me?" Mary Louise asks pointedly.

"No, of course not. It's just... this whole situation is bizarre," Aria says, glancing around the room.

"Why would someone warn you about your father but do nothing to prevent the danger?"

"Perhaps they're unable to intervene," Mary Louise suggests softly.

"Maybe," Aria concedes. "But if they're wealthy, they typically have the means to do much more!"

James' eyes widen as his mouth opens. The three look at him, puzzled. "Now I remember something odd that happened yesterday!"

"What?" Aria asks quickly.

"As I was leaving your house after delivering the milk, I noticed a person on the other side of the street standing in the shadows. The weird thing is that he was still there when my shift ended hours later."

Aria and Liam grin. "What did he look like? Did you notice anything special about him?" Liam urges.

"It was hard to see his face with his hat, but he had red hair and was, I would say, six feet tall. Normal corpulence," James ponders, then snaps his fingers. "I know! He had this unusual ring with a compass design worn over his glove. An odd thing to have."

"Are you sure it was a compass?" Mary Louise asks.

"Yes, I am certain. I saw it clearly because a ray

of sunshine illuminated it. Yesterday was sunny—a rarity we cherish in London," he adds as Aria and Liam nod, relating to their own experiences. "The sun caught his ring, and it sparkled brilliantly."

"Do you know this ring?" Liam asks Mary Louise.

"Freemasons wear golden rings with a compass on them," the girl replies.

"Freema-what?" Liam questions, his nose twitching.

"Of course!" Aria exclaims, tapping her forehead with her fingertips. "Your father is a Freemason!"

"Was," Mary Louise clarifies. "Years ago, my father left the Catholic Church and became a spiritualist. He thought joining the Freemasons would offer him a deeper understanding of the spiritual realm and its mysteries. But he didn't find what he wanted and quit after a few years."

Liam's eyes widen with curiosity. "What's this Freemason group?"

"The Freemasons are an ancient and discreet organization. You must be invited to join and participate in special ceremonies. Members swear to keep society's secrets and support one another. It's selective, so not just anyone can join. They value personal development, ethical living, and helping the community. However, they're quite private about their activities," Aria explains.

"You forgot to mention it's reserved for men!" Mary Louise says, her tone laced with disapproval.

Liam leans back, absorbing this new information. "That does sound interesting!"

"Maybe you can apply." Aria teases with a playful smile, eliciting a grimace from him. She turns to Mary Louise. "But do you think they're behind this?"

Mary Louise pauses, lost in thought. "It's possible. They're known for being very secretive."

"Thank you, James," Liam says, typing notes into his phone. "We'll handle it from here." The boy breathes a sigh of relief.

Aria suddenly jolts. "Now, let's go interrogate your parents."

"Right, but we can't just walk downstairs—they'll realize we snuck in... And I'm not keen on getting arrested again!" Liam intervenes.

James grins, finding their company more and more enjoyable. "Just follow me down the pipe and ring the bell," he suggests. Liam looks skeptical, peering out the window. The ground seems a long way down.

Mary Louise inhales deeply. "You're right. With my parents hosting a big dinner tonight, the house is bustling. You won't get through the servants' quarters unseen. But if you follow James and use the bell, I'll handle it. I'll tell my father we're all in French classes and have a project to discuss. I'll convince my mother to let you stay. Leave it to me."

"But didn't they ground you?" Aria asks.

"My father insists I improve my French, so he will be thrilled. He might even remove my punishment for something like this."

"As long as he doesn't ask me to speak French!" Liam laughs.

"Indeed, that would be messy! French class is not where you shine the most," Aria chimes in.

Liam gasps, "Ar—."

"Brilliant, it's decided then. Let's go, mates!" James exclaims, moving toward the window. "Follow me!" He swings his legs out, gripping the windowsill, and then vanishes with a thud as he lands on the pipe alongside the house.

Aria and Liam poke their heads out the window to find a lush garden below them. James waves at them as soon as he drops to the ground.

"We might not land in one piece!" Liam declares before looking at Aria, doubt filling her expression.

CHAPTER 7
THE MOST FAMOUS AUTHOR

Aria bounces in place, readying her body for the climb. She breathes loudly and follows James's path, replicating his actions with assurance. Her heart rate increases as she feels tingling in her hands and legs. The lightness of her dress does not protect her from the chilly breeze, the shiver increasing her sweat. The rain has ceased, but the damp surface challenges her grip. Taking a deep breath, she cautiously places her hands on the drain-pipe and gently lifts her right leg with a twist. Closing her eyes tightly, she thrusts her left leg and grabs the pipe like a monkey. Suppressing a shout of triumph, she slides down the pipe and lands silently beside James.

Liam peers down from the window. Aria urges

him to follow. He hesitates, shakes his head, and blows loudly to prepare himself. He looks at Mary Louise, who nods encouragingly.

Taking his place on the windowsill, he looks down, his heart pounding. "Just like the Branch BounceFlyer," he mutters, thinking of the tree acrobatics activity they practice back in Sommetville. He reaches for the wet drainpipe, recoils, then steels himself. *If Aria did it,* he thought, *I could do it too.*

He jumps forward, his expression fierce and determined, and grabs the pipe tightly. He rushes down, his jacket making noise as it tears apart until he lands next to Aria and James with a yelp.

Aria refrains from laughing as she gives him a hand. "You are quite the acrobat, my dear Liam!"

"Very funny!" he retorts, attempting to look at his back to see the damage.

"Let's go now!" James cuts in, already heading to the front of the house.

As they round the corner, a voice pierces the air.

"James! Where have you been?" a woman calls from the top of a stair leading to the underground. Her hair is neatly pinned in a bun, with one strand slipping out.

James stops abruptly, Aria and Liam crashing

into him. He straightens his jacket. "I was on my way to you, Mrs. Whittlesby."

"I hope so! We have a dinner to prepare and no time to waste! Meet me in the kitchen, please," the woman orders before disappearing into the servant's quarters without even acknowledging Aria and Liam.

James sighs before turning to the adventurers with a resigned look. "Sorry, mates, duty calls. I've got milk to deliver and will be in trouble if it's late." He walks around the corner where his cart of milk bottles stands. "The entrance you need is there!" He points toward the porch. "I'll see you later!" He grabs a bottle and dashes off, leaving the duo to their task.

"You can tell me whatever you want. This is a weird job!" Liam says as he looks at James pushing his cart.

Aria sighs heavily. "Not everyone in history is rich. Actually, most people are not."

Liam winces before drooping his shoulders. "Alright, Aria! It's our turn to step up and do our job," he says, heading to the porch. Aria can't help but laugh at the sight of his torn tweed jacket.

"What's so funny?" Liam asks, puzzled.

"You still manage to look distinguished! *Very*

chic!" she teases, trying to fix the tear. Liam inspects the damage and groans, "Why am I always the one with outfit problems?"

Aria's amusement is abruptly halted by the sound of the entrance door swinging open. A neatly dressed man with a well-groomed mustache that curls up at the ends steps out. He places his hat atop his head with a graceful movement. His hair is neatly combed to one side, and his almond-shaped eyes look sharp. His straight nose complements his structured face. He's dressed in a sharp, dark suit with a notched suitcoat, his white shirt crisp underneath. A pocket square adds a dash of sophistication to his outfit.

He pauses, noticing Aria and Liam in the entryway. His face breaks into a welcoming smile as he approaches.

"What a surprise. Who do I have the pleasure to meet?" he asks with a soft grin.

Aria is speechless, mesmerized by the man she admires so much. Liam catches her gaze, expecting her to jump into her usual role of introduction leader, but she's spellbound. He steps in, clearing his throat.

"Mary Louise is our friend and classmate. We

are working together on a project for our French class."

The man's expression shifts with intrigue. "That's wonderful! I continually hear Mary Louise speak of her French studies with little enthusiasm. I am glad she has friends to work on it with her. I'm afraid she hasn't embraced my fondness for the language and culture."

Liam flashes a brilliant smile. "Exactly! We're quite passionate about all things French, right, Aria?" He nudges her, making her jump out of her reverie.

Je suis ravi que vous veniez donner l'amour de cette langue à ma fille, the author says with a perfect French accent.

Liam scrunches up his face, his forehead creasing as he tries to think of a French reply. "O-o-ui," he mutters, the only French word he knows.

"We are... Sir Conan Doyle...' Aria stumbles over her words. 'I apologize; it's just I'm a huge admirer of your work! I LOVE Sherlock Holmes!' Liam gives an amused, slightly exasperated sigh as Aria turns into a fanatical creature. Soon, she might even ask him for an autograph!

The author smiles kindly. "Thank you, Miss—"

"Aria!" she blurts out.

"Miss Aria and you are...?" He looks at Liam.

"Liam, sir."

"Well, Miss Aria and Mr. Liam, it's a pleasure to have you here assisting Mary Louise. I must be off. My guests won't appreciate being kept waiting. My wife will be here to greet you."

"Thank you, sir," Liam replies promptly. Sir Conan Doyle tips his hat slightly in farewell.

Liam, unsure of the proper etiquette, hastily mimics a bow, eliciting a subtle smile from the author. The man departs, turning right onto the bustling street.

"A bow?" Aria teases, shaking her head in amusement.

"What? I don't own a hat, and how should I know the proper way to say goodbye here? They speak and behave as if they're in a play!"

Aria can't help but laugh, finding Liam's description spot-on. "You'll be even more out of your element if we ever go to France, Liam!"

"And you think you would do better?"

"*Je peux par-parler le français*," she attempts, her pronunciation faltering.

Liam raises an eyebrow, arms crossed, as he gazes at her skeptically.

Aria's grin fades as she suddenly realizes Doyle has left. "We need to follow him!"

Liam is taken aback at her sudden proposal. "We can't, Aria! Mary Louise is waiting for us, and how are we supposed to manage this outside world without someone from here?" he argues.

"We've done it before!" Aria insists, grabbing his arm and pulling him toward the street. "Come on, Dr. Watson. It's time to make history!"

"Dr. Watson? I'm Sherlock Holmes!" Liam protests.

"Roles are already decided, Liam. This isn't the time to argue!"

"But there's always time to—"

"Miss Aria and Mr. Liam?" a stern voice calls from behind.

They stop and turn to face the porch, where a tightly dressed man stands as straight as a stick. His shiny bald head and expressionless face give him an air of authority.

CHAPTER 8
THE LETTERS

The man at the door points for them to come inside. Aria and Liam exchange a worried glance, their faces tight. How did he know they were here?

Taking cautious steps toward the house, they startle as they see Mary Louise bursting onto the porch, her expression blending joy and concern. "Aria! Liam! I've been waiting for you!" she says, eliciting a disapproving look from the butler. "Thank you, Clifford. I'll take them to see Mama," she says, urging her friends to follow her.

As Aria steps in, she is astonished by the grandiosity of the entry. Its ceiling looms overhead with a dazzling chandelier twinkling in its center. The majestic staircase leading to the upper floors features an elegantly carved wood banister. Along it lies a marble table crowned with a white statue of the goddess Athena. The walls are covered with paintings depicting individuals from various historical periods. The red and blue flowery carpet flows across the floor, creating an inviting yet sophisticated atmosphere.

"We just saw your father outside," Liam says, leaning in as his jacket pulls tight across his shoulders. "Maybe we should've thought of a better story than the French class—it's not convincing!"

"Speak for yourself, Liam!" Aria retorts, lifting her chin and relaxing her shoulders.

Liam stares at her, bewildered. "Are you serious? You hardly said a word to him!"

Before Aria can reply, Mary Louise urges them, "We must follow my father! I know where he is going, but first, we must face my mother."

Without leaving time for the duo to respond, she quickly enters an opulent living room. Despite the heaviness of the use of velvet and gold, the place is cozy, with thick curtains at the windows and fluffy rugs on the floor. There's a fireplace made of marble and armchairs covered in velvet with soft cushions. The floors are so polished you can almost see your face, and a chandelier filled with candles sparkles above, making everything feel friendly and warm.

"Mama!" Mary Louise calls, causing her mother to look up from her book in surprise.

"I thought we asked you to stay in your room," Louisa quickly says before changing her expression to one of displeasure when she sees Aria and Liam standing in the hallway.

"I know, but my friends Aria and Liam from French class are here for our project."

Louisa inspects the guests with an intense evaluation that makes them squirm uncomfortably. She then redirects her gaze to her daughter. "I don't recall hearing about this project. And considering your actions this morning..."

"You must remember," Mary Louise interjects, her hand waving towards a desk holding an open letter set. "You were busy writing a letter here, and Father was reading the newspaper there." She points to a grand armchair across the room. "It was only two days ago."

Louisa's brow furrows. "Perhaps, but that doesn't change that you're grounded."

Mary Louise's posture softens, and a look of earnest regret fills her face. "I'm truly sorry, Mama." She averts her eyes, her fingers nervously entwining.

"I think the move to London has been unsettling. That's why I believe working on this project with my friends will help."

Louisa maintains her stare before relaxing her facial muscles. "Your father might be pleased to see your interest in French. You may go..." A spark of joy illuminates Mary Louise's expression. "But," her mother interjects, holding up a finger, "you'll wait for Nurse Penny. You're not to go out unchaperoned."

"Mama, I—"

"Lady Doyle," Aria interrupts with a charming smile, "our own governess is just outside. She didn't want to intrude on your lovely home."

Liam grimaces slightly, then straightens, slipping into a dramatic persona. "Absolutely. Our Nanny is always with us," he says, raising his hand in front of his heart, the motion tearing further through his jacket. He winces at the sound.

Aria suppresses a giggle. "We assure you, Lady Doyle, we'll be perfectly safe."

Louisa rises, using the armrest for support. "Very well." She looks at her daughter. "But remember, there are guests coming tonight, and you must return before supper—"

"We will, Mama," Mary Louise says as she

swishes around. They manage a quick bow of goodbye before Mary Louise rushes them out.

They speed out of the room, zooming past the startled butler Clifford in a frenzy. His worry over Mary Louise's disregard for protocol and what it might imply for her future lingers as they quickly escape from the house.

$$\mathrm{Q}$$

MARY LOUISE LEADS THE WAY. The hustle and bustle of the London streets force them to slow down as they blend into the foot traffic on the sidewalk.

Aria, walking briskly beside her, dodges a woman with a stroller. "Do you know where your father went?"

"Yes! He is meeting his friend Dr. Watson at his club," Mary Louise answers.

Liam exchanges a glance with Aria. "Dr. Watson? Like from the Sherlock Holmes stories?"

"Yes, he's a close friend of my father's. They were in the Freemasons together."

"That's interesting!" Liam thinks out loud. "But is he like the Dr. Watson in the book?"

"Yes and no. Authors often get inspired by the people in their lives to create their characters,"

Mary Louise explains as they turn onto a quieter street.

"Be careful, Liam! I might use you in my future stories!" Aria jokes.

"Do you want to become a writer?" Mary Louise asks, grinning.

Aria shakes her head vigorously and replies, "No way! Storytelling is fun, but I suck at writing and make a ton of spelling errors. I'm dyslexic, so English classes have been pretty much my worst nightmares!"

"At least you come up with funny expressions!" Liam cheers her up.

"I think I've heard of that," Mary Louise says as she touches her chin, trying to remember where she had heard this term. "Anyway, it shouldn't stop you. My father was a doctor before being an author, and he says that the story should always come first when writing. Don't let anything stop you from doing what you love!" She halts her stride and points down the street at an imposing building with pillars and a shiny statue on the front.

"That's the Athenaeum Club, a gentleman club for those in medicine and literature. Dr. Watson is a member."

Liam frowns. "But if it's a men's club, how will we get in?"

Aria grins, a mischievous glint in her eye. "We might have to bend a few rules."

They rush across the street, weaving through the traffic.

The trio quietly positions themselves behind the bushes lining the Athenaeum Club's entrance.

Aria leans toward Liam. "You should sneak in and find him," she says with urgency.

Liam glances from her to the club's guarded doorway, hesitating. "I'm not sure—"

"Shh!" Mary Louise cuts in, her finger directing their gaze to the door. "There's my father with Dr. Watson," she whispers. They crouch lower, using the foliage for cover as the two men come into earshot.

"Thank you for your advice, James," Sir Doyle says, pausing just off the curb.

"It's what I'm here for. But remember, threats like these should be taken seriously. You should obey their wish." Dr. Watson takes a handkerchief nicely folded inside his jacket's pocket. He quietly blows his nose, avoiding his friend's glance.

"Indeed, James. I'll see you at tonight's dinner, and let's keep this matter between us for now. My wife has enough to worry about."

"I will." James smiles.

Dr. Watson tips his hat, then steps into a waiting carriage, offering a final wave to Sir Doyle, who stays on the sidewalk. After putting back his hat on his head, the author turns and heads toward his home.

CHAPTER 9
A FAMILY AFFAIR

The group is quiet for a moment, their faces filled with shock. A loud whistle from behind startles them. The doorman of the nearby building is glaring at them intently. "May I ask what you're doing here?" he inquires.

They all rise to their feet, speechless. Mary Louise stammers something indecipherable.

"We're looking at your flowers!" Aria blurts, startling everyone. She steps toward the doorman, who towers over her from his spot on the porch. "How beautiful!" she says, her face lighting up before frowning as she notices there are no flowers. "Green shrubs are the way to go!" she adds hastily.

The doorman leans in closer. "Move along before I call your chaperones!"

They scamper off the lawn to the safety of the sidewalk, speeding away without looking back. They halt at the next corner when they spot Doyle scanning the area. They hurry to hide behind a parked carriage just before he looks in their direction.

"My father is being blackmailed," Mary Louise says, her voice trembling.

"We need to find these letters quickly," Aria says, peeking past the carriage to see if Doyle is still there. Seeing him walk on, she signals the others to get up. "We can stop this before it gets worse. If we find the letters, we can find who is behind this," she urges as they trail at a safe distance behind the author.

Mary Louise nods in agreement. "You're right."

"Do you have any idea where he could've concealed them?" Liam asks.

"They're probably in his office. It's his private space. Even my mother can't enter when he's not there. We can look during the dinner tonight. No one will come bothering us!"

"That's our chance," Aria says, eyes fixed ahead.

Liam frowns. "Doesn't it strike you as odd that his friend doesn't try to do more about the blackmail?"

"It's suspicious," Aria replies sharply. "No one dismisses blackmail so easily unless they don't care!"

"But remember, he's associated with the Freemasons. They get threatened often," Mary Louise adds.

"True, but your dad left the group. And if James is correct, one of them was spying on your house yesterday," Aria says. This idea sends shivers down Mary Louise's spine.

"Maybe that's why he is telling him to obey the blackmail. He is also behind this!" Liam adds.

"The man James saw had red hair," Mary Louise recalls.

"Yes, but they are a group. It could be a conspiracy!" Aria insists.

Mary Louise is lost in her thoughts as they arrive at her house and come to a stop. A thick silence falls upon them as they wait for her father to enter the home. Aria shifts restlessly, barely concealing her excitement to keep moving. Her eyes wander around the area. Across the street sits a park, just one of the many green spaces that give London its vibrant character. High society women, accompanied by their nannies and children, rush toward the entrance, enjoying their day.

"We've waited long enough. Let's head inside," Mary Louise says, stepping toward the porch.

"Hold on!" Liam interrupts. "What excuse will we give your parents for returning? We couldn't have possibly finished this project in such a short period! And we need to be able to stay tonight."

Mary Louise halts, a puzzled look crossing her face. "I hadn't considered that."

"He's got a point. We need a believable story," Aria says.

They exchange glances, all deep in thought. "Got it!" Mary Louise exclaims. "We'll say your Nanny hurt herself, and since your parents are out of London on vacation, you have nowhere to stay. We'll tell them they went to the French Riviera, very common at this time of year."

Liam grimaces. "Why would our parents leave us behind?"

Mary Louise looks at him in disbelief. "It's not unusual for parents to travel without their children."

Liam looks up at her, confused.

"Listen, Liam," Aria says quickly. "Back in the day, it was perfectly normal for parents to go on a trip without their kids. It wasn't frowned upon like it is now."

"The more I travel to the past, the more I enjoy Sommetville!"

"Yes..." Aria sighs. "But the tricky part is pretending we're siblings. We don't really look like we come from the same family..."

Mary Louise chuckles. "You might not look alike, but you definitely bicker like siblings."

Aria and Liam startle in surprise, both looking towards each other. "Maybe we could say that Liam's parents passed away due to the Asian flu," Aria suggests, "and my family took him in."

"That's simple enough to remember," Liam concedes.

Their conversation is abruptly stopped as Nanny Penny appears suddenly from behind, making Mary Louise gasp. "What are you doing here, Miss Mary Louise?" the Nanny inquires sternly.

"Nanny Penny!" She turns to face her. "These are my friends, Aria and Liam."

The Nanny stares at them, giving Liam's suit a particularly hard look. "Why are you out without a chaperone?"

"We didn't go out alone!" Aria quickly interjects, bursting into tears. Liam's brow furrows in confusion as he watches her cry. "Our nanny fell ill, and we rushed here after the doctor arrived and took her to the hospital!" Aria cries, her face buried in her hands. Despite her stern demeanor, Nanny Penny softens at the girl's distress. "We're so fond of her," Aria adds, evoking a sympathetic reaction from the Nanny.

Aria nudges Liam, who lets out a wail before covering his face to mimic crying. "Awful!" he shouts, attracting the attention of passersby.

Mary Louise wraps an arm around Aria. "Exactly, Nanny Penny. We were working on a project at their place when the unthinkable happened. I can't imagine how I'd cope if it were you!" she says, noticing a flicker of happy surprise on her Nanny's face.

Without further ado, Nanny Penny motions for them to follow her into the house. Aria drops her facade and goes after Mary Louise. Meanwhile, Liam's exaggerated cries trail behind them until he looks up, realizing he's been left alone on the sidewalk.

He hurries to catch up. "Am I not the best actor of all time?"

"Come on, you almost alerted the whole street!"

Before Liam can speak, Mr. Clifford appears, silencing him. Nanny Penny leads the way into the house, and the trio follows, trying not to attract attention as they pass the watchful butler.

As they reach the living room, the faint sound of Mr. and Mrs. Doyle's discussion reaches their ears.

"Nurse Penny," Sir Doyle exclaims, surprised to

see her with the three children in tow. "Have you already finished your French project?"

Mary Louise doesn't allow her Nanny to speak and launches into the fabricated story. Her parents' expressions cycle from shock to concern as she narrates, with Aria and Liam adding their dramatic flair. "So, as you can see, they have nowhere to go until their parents return. Would it be alright if they stay here?"

Louisa and her spouse exchange an understanding look before swiftly scrutinizing the two visitors. "They may stay. But we must contact their parents promptly," Louisa says as she looks at her butler. "Clifford, please make the call."

"Of course, my Lady."

"Remember, we are hosting tonight, so you must keep to the nursery," Louisa adds as she stands up.

"Thank you, Mama!" Mary Louise exclaims, embracing her mother.

"And we'll expect a full introduction to our guests tomorrow," Sir Doyle says, smiling and glancing at the pair.

"We'll give Clifford all the details, I promise! And, of course, Papa! But we really should get back to our project," Mary Louise says. Before her parents can reconsider, the three depart the room hastily. Liam almost trips as he walks backward to hide his tired suit.

At the foot of the stairs, Nanny Penny stops them. "Could I have your address and the name of the hospital where your nanny is being treated?"

"Uh," Aria fumbles.

"We will give everything to Clifford as promised, Nanny," Mary Louise jumps in quickly. "But we really must finish our homework first." She signals her friends to follow her up the stairs.

Nanny Penny watches them go, suspicion dawning on her. "They were much sadder earlier. Something tells me Miss Mary Louise isn't being entirely truthful about these two," she whispers to herself, eyes lingering on the children as they disappear upstairs.

CHAPTER 10

FANCY DINNER = FANCY SUSPECTS

W hen the three of them enter the nursery, Mary Louise heads to her desk and grabs a blank sheet of paper that she places at its center. She gestures to Aria to sit, who promptly takes the fountain pen. She dips the pen's nib into the inkwell, ready to write.

"Let's go through what we know!" Aria says.

"It started when I got a letter with no return address that said my dad was in danger," Mary Louise recalls.

"I still don't understand why you are the one who received this letter," Aria thinks aloud before committing the detail to the paper.

"Maybe because they knew I would do something to save him!"

"Maybe…" Aria whispers.

"Someone with red hair, of average height, and wearing a glove with a ring from this secret group was snooping around the house," Liam adds.

"The Freemasons," both girls say simultaneously.

Liam nods in agreement. "Yeah, the Freemasons."

Aria follows up as she writes aloud, "And your dad's being blackmailed, but his friend Watson thinks he should give in to the blackmail, which is strange." Aria ponders out loud, looking at her notes, "Maybe the kidnappers are after something to do with your father's past involvement in the Freemasons. But he's not a member anymore, so it doesn't make sense unless no one knows he quit?" She turns to Mary Louise and asks, "Could that be it?"

Mary Louise's expression grows serious. "It's possible. They're secretive, so who knows?"

Aria and Liam consider this. It's a significant detail.

"Maybe it's someone with a grudge against the Freemasons," Liam suggests.

"Then why target only your dad?" Aria challenges, trying to piece the mystery together.

"It's possible others were warned too," Mary

Louise suggests.

"Or the Freemasons are silencing your father for something he knows!" Liam proposes.

"That is a possibility. It could also be an angry fan who wants revenge for killing Sherlock Holmes!" Aria adds.

"But it's been already almost a decade since that happened! Why act now?" Mary Louise steps in.

"We need to find the blackmail letters to know what they are asking! Until then, it will be—" Aria stops as the doorbell rings.

Mary Louise urges, "We need to go downstairs. The guests are arriving!"

⚲

THE GROUP quickly hurries through the corridors, their footsteps reverberating off the walls. As they reach the top of the last set of stairs, Mary Louise signals them to stop. This is the perfect spot to observe the entrance hall without being seen.

Mr. Clifford greets a couple, both dressed in their finest attire. The woman has a light complexion, and her hair is done up into a perfectly pinned bun. She wears a stunning lavender gown with detailed embroidery that nips in at her waist. When she turns around, Clifford helps her out of her luxurious fur coat. The man follows her lead, looking just as fashionable in his suit, and they move to the reception room.

"That's Baroness Orczy and her husband, Montague MacLean Barstow," Mary Louise informs her friends in a hush. "She's an up-and-coming author who writes mystery novels like my father."

Aria, peering through the railing, gestures excitedly. "Look! She's carrying something."

Liam squints for a better view. "Seems like a leather briefcase."

"Yes, I overheard my dad mentioning he would assist her with her novel. Perhaps she's brought a draft for him to read!" Mary Louise says.

The doorbell's echo halts their speculations. After ushering the couple in, Mr. Clifford hurries back to greet the next guests. Their hearts skip as Dr. Watson steps inside, handing his hat to the butler.

Liam whispers skeptically, "I've got a bad feeling about him. He's involved. I just know it!"

Mary Louise twitches her pursed lips. "But he's always been around, helping my father..."

"People can surprise you, Mary Louise," Aria says. "Sometimes, those who seem kind have the darkest secrets."

Error

 ✳ 80 ✳

Their conversation stops as the doorbell rings again. Mr. Clifford, now sweating profusely, rushes back to attend to the new guests. "Sir Montgomery, Lady Harrington, welcome," he greets, bowing slightly. The couple is silent, offering their backs for the butler to take their coats.

"Are Sir and Lady Doyle in the reception room?" Sir Montgomery asks, his gaze fixed forward.

"Yes, sir. They await you for the cocktail," Mr. Clifford responds, directing them to the party.

Mary Louise leans closer to her friends. "That's Sir Montgomery and Lady Harrington. He's one of the most successful art dealers. He is American but recently moved to England after marrying Lady Harrington, the daughter of the esteemed Lord Harrington."

Aria and Liam watch in awe as Sir Montgomery gallantly offers his arm to his wife. There is something mesmerizing about him.

Liam looks puzzled, trying to figure out the complex social structure of the past. "So, he has a title now?"

Mary Louise nods, smiling slightly. "Many wealthy Americans seek out titled English spouses. It's about the prestige of old money for them."

"They marry for status, not love?" Liam asks, his frown deepening.

"Once again, you've got to pay more attention in history class, my dear Liam. Marriages of convenience or for financial gain weren't uncommon in the past," Aria explains with a hint of exasperation.

"That was often the case, but times have been changing since Queen Victoria's era," Mary Louise says. "My parents married for love, and I plan to do the same."

A quiet moment passes as they watch Clifford lead the couple to the reception hall. "Everyone's arrived," Mary Louise says as she stands. "Let's go to my father's office!"

"Wait!" Liam intervenes, getting to his feet. "We could listen to their conversation. It is an opportunity we don't want to miss!" The sound of loud conversations and a piano carry through the air.

"You're right," Aria says before turning to Mary Louise. "Is there a safe way for us to spy?"

"There is always a way in a house like this one." Mary Louise smiles. "Follow me, but keep quiet! If my parents find us, we will be in big trouble. Kids are not allowed in parties like this one!" She walks down the stairs and leads them to a room adjacent to the festivities.

As Aria walks into what appears to be the library, a smile spreads across her face. The floor-to-ceiling bookshelves overflow with leather-bound books of every size and color imaginable. She inhales deeply, filling her lungs with the sweet aroma of paper that never fails to comfort her.

Mary Louise circles around the center of the room and stops before a pair of wooden doors. She cautiously slides one open, and the sound of the reception wafts into the library. Aria and Liam join her, their ears carefully placed against the tiny opening.

"That's truly magnificent!" they overhear Baroness Orczy exclaim.

"All thanks to William. When he showed me that painting, I was so taken with it that now I bring it wherever I travel," Arthur Doyle responds, mingling with the piano playing.

"I've got a new collection arriving from New York soon, Baroness Orczy. You should visit my gallery to see it. There's an artist, Mary Cassatt, whose impressionist work of mothers and children is quite remarkable," Lord Montgomery says.

"I'll make a point to do so," the Baroness responds with interest.

Their conversation is interrupted by the clink of cutlery against glass. "My dear friends!" Arthur Doyle's voice booms. "My wife and I are thrilled to host you this evening. Not only did I wish for you to meet each other, but I also have an exciting announcement." The room fills with eager murmurs. "As many of you know, I once decided to end Sherlock Holmes' adventures, not anticipating the outcry it would cause. The shadow of Holmes had grown too heavy on me. Yet, the calls for his return have persisted, even after a decade. So, I've chosen to revive him and continue his tales."

The revelation sends a wave of astonishment and delight through the crowd, manifesting itself in a chorus of applause.

"My dear Baroness Orczy, it sounds like you will have competition again," Dr. Watson says.

The room stays silent for a moment. "Nonsense!" the Baroness replies. "We authors are not competing with each other. There are merely not enough books to satisfy all the avid readers out there. This is a fantastic news!"

"I am glad you are all thrilled. I had confessed it to my dear friend Lord Montgomery and could not wait to share the news with everyone. Let's now go enjoy our dinner!" Sir Doyle concludes, leading the way into the dining room.

Mary Louise steps back from the door, closing it gently. "I had no idea!"

"You didn't know?" Liam looks at her, surprised.

"He must have only just decided."

Aria rises; her steps are quick and restless. "This is odd," she murmurs, thinking out loud.

"What's odd?" Mary Louise steps closer, concerned.

Aria pauses a severe look on her face. "In our time, Sir Conan Doyle never brought Sherlock Holmes back. I wonder if..." She trails off, the implication hanging in the air.

"Could that be the motive for the threats against him?" Liam suggests, finishing her thought.

Aria nods, her mind racing with the implications of this unexpected turn of events.

CHAPTER II
AN AUTHOR'S OFFICE

M ary Louise slowly moves away from Aria and Liam, her gaze fixed on the void. Could Aria be right? Could the revival of Sherlock Holmes be the reason?

Her thoughts are cut short as Mr. Clifford suddenly bursts into the library, startling them all.

"What are you doing here?" he demands, his piercing gaze sweeping over each of them. An oppressive stillness fills the air.

Mary Louise steps toward the butler with confidence. "I was just showing our guests the library." Clifford squints at Aria and Liam, who are glued to the reception hall. "We were just leaving. Aria, Liam, let's head back to the nursery!" She heads to the exit, Aria and Liam rushing toward her. They offer the butler a timid smile as they pass.

The trio hurries, nearly bumping into a servant carrying food. They take the stairs two at a time without looking back. Mary Louise leads the charge. "Quick, to my father's office!" she urges. They dash through the hallways, passing countless doors.

"Why do ancient houses have to be so big?" Liam pants, trying to catch his breath.

"They're for hosting big parties with lots of friends!" Aria says, her smile wide as she pictures the grand celebrations these walls have seen.

Mary Louise takes a quick look around before gently pushing the door open. As they walk into the author's office, they are at once drawn to the chaos in the room. The massive desk in front of them is made entirely of wood, but it's unclear where one would write because it's covered with a large pile of papers and an inkwell that has seen better times. The shelves around the room are packed with loose papers.

"I suddenly feel less guilty about my bedroom," Liam remarks, grimacing at the disarray.

"At least he has a reason; he's a writer! You're just untidy," Aria teases, scanning the papers on the desk.

"As if you're any tidier!"

"I don't go around judging, though," Aria says with a playful glance. "Are you going to help or just make remarks about the mess?" She raises an eyebrow, prompting a resigned sigh from Liam.

They work together, combing through the room for the elusive blackmail letters. They sift through each document in silence until Aria exclaims triumphantly.

"I think I've got one!" she announces, waving a small card. Mary Louise and Liam abandon their search to join her.

Mary Louise's expression falls as she reads. "This isn't a letter to my father. It's probably from his new book." She turns back to a cabinet to resume her hunt.

Aria bites her lip, giving the card another glance. "My bad, false alarm," she admits, setting it down.

"You're no Sherlock Holmes, my dear Aria," Liam teases.

"At least I found something," she snaps back, hands on her hips.

"Oh no, what—"

Mary Louise's gasp cuts them off. They freeze, their attention snapping to her as she holds up a small piece of paper.

"Did you find something?" Aria's voice quivers with anticipation.

Mary Louise looks up from the paper, her eyes brimming with tears. She tries speaking but can't find the words. Silently, she offers the paper to her friends.

Liam reads the bold lettering aloud:

> Stop what you're doing now,
> or bad things will happen to
> you and your family. This is
> your last warning.

Mary Louise buries her face in her hands, the tears she's been holding back streaming down her cheeks. The realization is too much—someone is indeed threatening her father.

Liam puts a comforting hand on her shoulder. "Hey, we'll figure this out. There's no need to cry. Your dad is safe now."

"But for how long?" Mary Louise sobs.

Aria grabs the note for a second look, her brow furrowing with determination. "I've got it!" she exclaims, causing Mary Louise to look up. "The note says your dad has to stop something to avoid trouble. We just have to persuade him to stop whatever they are asking!"

Liam gives Aria a skeptical look. "And you think he'll listen to us?"

Aria shrugs. "It's worth a try, but I don't think it'll be easy—"

Their conversation halts as the door flies open. Arthur Doyle stands tall, his initial shock quickly turning to anger. He clutches the leather case given by Baroness Orczy like a shield.

"May I ask what you are doing in my office?" he says gravely.

The three of them are speechless, caught in the act.

"Papa, I... They admire your work, and I just wanted to..." Mary Louise's explanation fades under her father's disapproving look.

"You know the rule about my office, Mary Louise," he says firmly, his disappointment evident.

Liam steps forward, his voice shaky. "Mr., uh, Sir Doyle, this isn't Mary Louise's fault. Aria and I... we dream of being writers, and we begged her to show us behind the scenes."

There is an intense silence as Arthur Doyle scrutinizes them. They hold their breath, awaiting his sentence. After what feels like an eternity, he points at them with his leather case. "We will discuss this tomorrow. Until then, I don't want to see you outside the nursery. Understood?"

The trio nods and exits the office, Mr. Doyle stepping aside to let them pass. At the threshold, Aria turns back to see Doyle placing the leather case in a drawer. "Sir Doyle," she calls, catching his attention. "You know..." She pauses, searching for the right words. "It would be incredible if Sherlock Holmes could return," she finally says, drawing a faint smile from the author.

Not waiting for an answer, she joins Mary Louise and Liam in the hallway. Silently, they make their way to the nursery.

"Why did you say that to him?" Liam asks Aria as they get back to the bedroom.

"I wanted to tell him to follow the letter's warning, but..." Aria trails off.

"You chickened out," Liam says with a teasing grin, which Aria answers with a sheepish nod.

"What could Papa be involved in to get such threats?" Mary Louise says, sinking onto her bed.

"Has he been acting differently lately?" Aria asks.

Mary Louise stares at the ceiling, thinking back. "No... He's been anxious, but that's probably because of Mama's illness," she says, her voice tinged with concern.

"Being blackmailed would make anyone anxious," Liam points out.

Aria sidesteps the obvious. "What's wrong with your mother?"

"She's had tuberculosis for years, which is why we left London for Undershaw," Mary Louise explains, her voice soft.

Aria offers a sympathetic smile before heading back to the desk, jotting down the new clue.

"Don't forget about Baroness Orczy being jealous of his work!" Liam reminds her.

Chewing on the pen, Aria considers this. "But the blackmail started before he announced his return to writing Sherlock Holmes stories tonight, right?"

Liam rubs his head, overwhelmed by the puzzle. "Yes, but..."

"Let's sleep on it and pick this up tomorrow,"

Mary Louise suggests, the day's events visibly weighing on her.

Agreeing, Aria settles into the bed opposite Mary Louise's, and Liam is guided to a separate room. After all, Nurse Penny would never approve of a boy staying in the girls' room, brother or not. That might be one too many things to make her endure.

CHAPTER 12
WHERE IS SIR ARTHUR CONAN DOYLE?

Clouds cast a dim light over the dining hall where Aria, Liam, and Mary Louise sit silently, the previous day's adventures still crowding their thoughts. As a maid tops off Liam's cup with hot chocolate, Louisa enters briskly, prompting Mr. Clifford to hurry over.

"I need this envelope sent out immediately," Louisa says, handing it to Clifford. "Sir Doyle had to leave for an urgent meeting early this morning."

"Right away, Lady Doyle," Clifford says, quickly departing.

Mary Louise stares at her mother. "Where did Papa go?" she asks, trying to conceal her quavering voice.

"He was called for a matter of urgency the first

hour in the morning. Nothing to worry about, of course," Louisa responds, making them freeze. "Mary Louise, your father informed me of yesterday's incident," she adds, disappointment lacing her tone. Aria and Liam cast their eyes downward. "I expect better behavior. London has been hard on you, and you are happy to have friends with you, but that is not an excuse."

"Yes, Mama," Mary Louise says, looking at her plate.

Louisa's gaze shifts to Aria and Liam. "When will your parents come for you?"

"Soon, Lady Doyle," Aria responds, avoiding eye contact.

"We were just going to work on our French," Mary Louise says, rising from her seat.

"That's wise. Nurse Penny will be in to check on you. You're not to leave the house," Louisa instructs.

The trio exits swiftly; heads bowed as they pass Louisa and return to the nursery, hearts pounding.

No sooner has she closed her bedroom door than Mary Louise exclaims through tears, "It's happening!"

"We don't know that," Liam tries to reassure her, though he sounds uncertain.

"We have to find him," Aria insists.

"But the city's massive!" Liam protests.

"We have to find more clues," Aria says.

Mary Louise calms her sobs, a new determination in her eyes. "James might have seen something on his deliveries."

"But we're supposed to stay here," Liam reminds them.

Mary Louise's expression hardens. "Then we will have to find a way to leave unnoticed. I'd face any punishment to save Papa."

Aria's eyes light up with a plan. "Just get me some paper," she tells Mary Louise, who quickly obliges. Aria grabs a pen and dips it in ink, starting to write a beautiful script.

Nanny Penny,

Aria and Liam had to make a trip to the hospital to see their beloved Nanny.

I am not feeling well, so I'm taking some time off to rest.

Aria sets the pen down and leaps from the chair, causing Liam to step aside. "Do you have any teddy bears? And maybe a doll with brown hair?" she asks Mary Louise urgently.

Mary Louise, puzzled, nods. "Yes, over there," she says, pointing to a trunk. Aria snatches them up and hurries to the bed.

"You can't be serious." Liam smiles, watching Aria arrange the bears under the blankets.

"What are you doing?" Mary Louise asks, bewildered.

"This is a trick we must do to save the world sometimes!" Aria says as she places the doll under the covers, arranging the hair to face the room. She beams with pride at her work.

"Maybe cover a little bit more of the doll," Liam suggests, prompting Aria to adjust the trick.

Aria looks one last time at the fake sick Mary Louise and beams. "Let's place this note on the door now!"

"On it!" Liam says. He is much more willing to break the rules when he knows his mother will never find out.

Mary Louise watches, a mix of emotions swirling within her as Aria brings her back to the moment. "We've got to move," Aria shouts, running towards the window. She's down the side of the building before the others come close, dropping to the ground with a soft thud. Liam follows, moving out of the window with better grace than before.

He stands, brushing off his hands with a self-satisfied smile. "Quite the adventurer, right?"

Mary Louise joins them, gesturing towards the dense bushes lining the wall. "Through there."

Liam grimaces at the sight of the thorns. "Are we sure about this?"

"There's no time to delay," Aria insists, making her way to a small gap in the foliage. She squeezes through the tight space, back pressed against the wall. Mary Louise and Liam follow, dodging thorns as they push through the bushes.

As they near the street, Aria halts, catching sight of a man approaching the house. She peers through the leaves, trying to get a better look. "Do you recognize him?" she whispers to Mary Louise.

Mary Louise peers through a tiny gap in the bushes but only catches Mr. Clifford welcoming the visitor. "I couldn't see his face."

"Look at his hair! And his hand!" Liam exclaims. The girl squints, spotting curly hair coming out of his hat and something bright gold glistening on his finger, a large ring with an embedded compass design.

"The same man James saw!" Aria whispers in awe.

"Should we wait for him to leave so we can question him?" Liam suggests quietly.

Before Aria can respond, James passes in front

of them, disappearing on the street. As she points him out, a thorn pricks her, making her shriek. "Ouch!"

"James!" Mary Louise exclaims, pushing Aria out of their hideout.

They dart from the bushes before quickly rushing into the street. Liam, lagging behind, stumbles into something solid as he comes out, crying out as pain shoots through his shin.

James' eyes brighten as he sees Liam. He drops his cart to hold his shoulder. "Liam! Are you alright?"

"I th-think so," the boy mutters, breathing fast so as not to cry.

"What are you guys doing here?" James asks in a whisper.

"We've got no time—my father was blackmailed, and he's gone!" Mary Louise blurts out. She quickly tells him everything they found out, glancing around to ensure no one can hear. "Will you help us?" she implores him with her gaze.

"Of course, I will, I just—"

"We need to get out of here," Aria interrupts, turning to Liam. "Can you walk?"

"I think so," Liam replies, his color slowly returning.

"I'm off to deliver milk to Lord Montgomery," James says, heading back to his cart.

"That's perfect," Aria chimes in. Everyone looks at her, puzzled. "You can gather information from the servants. They always know everything."

Mary Louise agrees, "Yes, servants are often the biggest gossips. It's kind of the perk of being one."

James nods. "Alright, I'll see what I can find out."

Aria, brimming with excitement, turns to Liam. "You'll go with James. Mary Louise and I will talk to Lord Montgomery and his wife. You're already dressed for the part," she says, noting his disheveled suit.

Liam looks down at his clothes. The day spent climbing and moving has only made his outfit worse. The stitch down the back of the jacket has given way entirely, and the one on his shorts is hanging by a thread, promising trouble if it snaps. "Fine, but next time, we switch roles," he says, extending his pinky.

Aria links her pinky with his. "Promise!"

James laughs softly at Aria and Liam's peculiar pinky swear. Mary Louise observes, fascinated by their customs, which become increasingly strange as she watches them interact.

The group starts moving, afraid that someone might hear them if they talk. Just a small distance away, they spot the lord's impressive mansion. The house boasts numerous square windows that look out at the neighborhood. At the center, a grand entrance door is framed by an elaborate circular window, while the walls are made of dark red bricks with bright white borders. Two tall brick chimneys reach up to the sky, giving an almost royal feeling to the home.

"We have arrived," Mary Louise says as Aria and Liam look at the mansion in awe.

"Is this a house?" Liam asks, his eyes wide in shock.

"Yes," Mary Louise says without emotion. She points to a tree near the street, "Let's meet by that tree once we are done!"

"Okay," Liam agrees, stepping towards the property.

James catches his arm, prompting him to stop. "Where are you going?"

Liam looks puzzled as he glances around. "Delivering the milk with you!" he replies, confused.

James giggles. "You are definitely not from this time, mate!" he laughs. "Do you really think we get to go in by the grand entrance?"

Liam frowns in incomprehension. James points toward a small metal gate at the end of the residence. "This is where people like me belong."

Liam's frown deepens, the era's social rules dawning on him.

"See you shortly," Mary Louise says, departing with Aria toward the porch.

Liam follows James toward the servants' entrance, staying as small and invisible as their status requires.

CHAPTER 13
THE MONTGOMERY MANSION

J ames passes Liam the glass milk bottles one by one. Eventually, Liam's arms become too full to handle any more and buckle under the weight of just a few bottles. James quickly scoops up six bottles into his own arms. Without effort, he goes down the stairs to the servants' quarters beneath the house. Meanwhile, Liam is sweating profusely from his attempt to check his movements. Unfortunately, his grip weakens as he reaches the last step, and a bottle slips away to crash loudly on the floor.

"Be careful!" a woman shouts as she approaches the crash scene. "Just so you know, James, we won't be paying for that." In her mid-fifties, the woman stands tall in a simple grey garment cascading to the ground. Her white apron is decorated with different colored stains and tied neatly at her waist.

"Understood, Mrs. Jones," James answers,

setting his bottles on a sturdy table. "My apologies. He's new and still learning."

"He'd better improve quickly or will be paying for his mistakes!" the cook says sternly, eyeing Liam, frozen on the stairway. With a stern face and piercing gaze, she turns to a girl slightly older than Liam, sweeping the floor. "Alice, deal with this mess now!"

James takes the rest of Liam's bottles while Alice comes closer with a broom to sweep up the pieces of glass.

"I'm really sorry," Liam whispers, helping her with the glass shards.

"Don't worry, it happens," she responds quietly, focused on her task.

"How long have you been working here?"

"Nearly two years. I started when I was twelve."

Liam gasps in shock. "Working at twelve? That's awful!" he blurts, earning a confused glance from Alice.

She looks at him, bewildered. "You're not much older, are you?"

He composes himself, feeling his facade slipping. "Well, yes, but I'm just delivering milk... It seems like you do a lot more."

Alice sighs. "As a girl, I had few options after the

orphanage. Some shops were hiring women, but not girls like me. And women are not allowed in the factory, so service was my only choice."

Before Liam can answer, James summons him. He sends Alice a comforting smile and strides away, leaving her to finish her job.

"I was just telling Mrs. Jones what happened at the Doyle residence!" James tells Liam excitedly. The cook fills two cups with tea, offering them to the boys without a word. Liam inhales the delicate scent of green tea wafting towards him, eagerly anticipating a refreshing sip after all these efforts.

"Do you think he's left his wife for good?" Mrs. Jones asks, her eyes twinkling with curiosity.

A woman wearing a spotless black dress and an immaculately placed apron enters the room. She has her hair pulled back in a neat knot. "Really, Mrs. Jones, you're not spreading rumors again, are you?" she asks with a playful scowl, then leans in with a sly smile. "So, what's the scoop? Anything interesting?"

"Sir Doyle has apparently left his home for good, leaving his wife behind, Miss Taylor," the cook quickly explains, causing the woman to gasp. Liam looks over at James, who gives him a subtle nod to remain silent.

"Where did you hear that? Can you be certain

it's true?" Miss Taylor probes. The cook nods towards James.

"It's the real deal. Liam and I just came from there, didn't we?" James says, sipping his tea as he glances at Liam.

Liam begins to utter words, but James' throat-clearing silences him. He doesn't wish to spread gossip; however, this could be their chance to get some information. Feeling everyone's eyes on him, he stammers, "Perhaps you've heard something?"

The two women straighten, eager to dive deeper into the conversation. "Well, it's not shocking. I over-heard her ladyship mention the Doyles' argument last night," shares Miss Taylor, catching Liam off-guard.

"Do we know the reason?" Mrs. Jones steps closer, her face alight with eagerness.

"Not sure, but it seems Sir Doyle is working on his next Sherlock Holmes novel," she reveals, drawing gasps from the gathered servants.

"A new Sherlock Holmes?" a young boy shining shoes pipes up.

"Exactly, and Lady Doyle isn't too pleased. Word is, she's weary of her husband's constant writing."

James catches Liam's eye, this revelation casting a new light on their investigation. James faces the two women. "Alright, I've shared my news. Now it's your turn. Spill this house gossip!"

Mrs. Jones, the cook, flashes a mischievous smile at Miss Taylor. "Come on now, you must have some juicy scoops to share! You're her ladyship's maid, after all!"

Miss Taylor gives back her wry smile and speaks quietly to the group. "I think Lord Montgomery is having money troubles."

Liam and James' mouths open in disbelief. Noticing their shock, Miss Taylor explains, "I overheard his lordship on the phone, talking about needing more paintings to 'cover costs.'" Liam and James look skeptical, prompting her to continue, "And right after that, I had to take back one of her ladyship's recent jewelry purchases." They all stare at her as she nods theatrically.

Their discussion is abruptly cut short by the arrival of a dapperly dressed man. "What's the meaning of this gathering? You're not paid to socialize," he says sharply before addressing Miss Taylor. "Her Ladyship requires you. Off you go."

Without a word, she leaves while Mrs. Jones returns to her duties. The house butler looks hard at Liam and James before exiting the kitchen.

Liam and James's minds are buzzing with their discoveries as they depart from the estate.

$\mathcal{Q}$

ARIA AND MARY LOUISE step into the grand entrance hall, as majestic as the house's exterior. The hall brims with elegant furniture and decorations, so much so that Aria struggles to take it all in. The brief wait outside has given them time to plan their visit. Their age, matching that of Montgomery's daughter Victoria, serves as their pretext for entry.

The footman escorts them to a library whose walls are covered with bookshelves with a cozy seating area at its center. Four grand windows offer a breathtaking view of the private garden. Mary Louise settles into an armchair, leaving Aria standing.

"Her Ladyship will be with you shortly," the footman informs them before leaving the room.

"We must hope Victoria isn't here. I don't like her and am unsure what to say to her...." Mary Louise murmurs to Aria.

"Why don't you like her?"

Mary Louise hunches her shoulders. "She's the perfect noblewoman: always smiling and watchful of her words. Everyone around here expects me to act just like her!" she says with a bemused grin before her expression falls again. "Aren't you going to sit down?"

Aria shyly walks toward one of the armchairs, nervously hovering on the edge of the seat. The chairs are plush and luxurious, almost intimidating to sit in. Her apprehension is short-lived, however, as an elegant woman enters. Her graceful demeanor and warm smile at once put them at ease.

"Miss Mary Louise, it's a delight to see you," she says, welcoming the girl, who rises smoothly from her seat. Seeing Aria perched uneasily on the edge of a chair, she moves closer. In a hasty move, Aria almost knocks over a side table. She takes a step back and gives an embarrassed curtsy as an apology.

"I understand you're here to see Victoria," the lady says gently, her voice free of judgment.

"Yes, is she here, my lady?" Mary Louise asks with a hopeful expression.

"She is, but she is taking her piano lesson and cannot stop. Perhaps there's another way I can assist?" Her gaze softens, touched with concern. "Can I help with something else? I was nearby yesterday when your parents were arguing. Is everything okay? We are always here to support you," she adds, taking Mary Louise's hand. The revelation leaves Mary Louise speechless.

The moment is shattered when the housemaster, Lord Montgomery, walks in. His shock at seeing unexpected guests is visible on his face. "I wasn't aware we had visitors," he says before greeting them with a head tilt. "Everything alright?" He looks at Aria. "I don't think we have met before."

Aria steps forward. "I'm Aria from——" She halts before making a mistake. "From the same school as your daughter. I mean, same class. We were looking to ask her some advice," she corrects herself, catching Mary Louise's anxious glance.

"Victoria is busy, I'm afraid. She is working hard to become the best piano player in the country," he responds, his smile holding a hint of suspicion.

"Since we're here, could we perhaps see some of the art you sell?" Aria asks, her request catching the lord off guard. "My parents adore art, and though they're traveling, they'd be excited to see some of your paintings. Mary Louise showed us the ones her parents bought from you; they are spectacular!" She says with a grandiose air, trying to sound posh and upper-class.

The lord straightens. "They're welcome to visit my gallery. It's only a stone away!"

Aria's puzzled look at the phrase 'a stone away' catches Mary Louise's attention, and she quickly comes to her help. "We'd love to, my lord. We know it is close to here, but maybe you have some paintings to show Aria so she can talk to her parents?"

Lord Montgomery hesitates. "Well, if you are so eager, come to my office. I have the photographs of all our catalogs. You can have a look while you wait for Victoria." The girls light up at the opportunity. "Will you join us, dear?" he asks his wife, who declines with a decisive shake of her head.

With that, they move from the library toward the room Aria and Mary Louise are most eager to see.

CHAPTER 14

AN ODD FEELING

L ord Montgomery leads Aria and Mary Louise through the numerous passageways of his estate. Paintings depicting the long noble line of his wife's family watch over the corridors. He strides confidently into his office, where a beautiful marble desk with wonderfully crafted golden legs stands prominently in the room. To the right, bookshelves line the wall, while the left side boasts a small arrangement of lavishly decorated armchairs and a couch.

He walks over to his desk and opens a drawer, removing a set of black-and-white photographs he offers to Aria. "These showcase the current paintings available for purchase, with prices noted on the back," he explains to Aria, who scrutinizes the images. Her eyes widen at the sight of renowned works, many capturing the essence of the Art Nouveau period.

"Thank you so much, my lord, for showing us these," Mary Louise says, buying Aria time to examine the photographs closely.

"It's my pleasure," Lord Montgomery smiles. He turns his attention to Aria. "I look forward to meeting your parents, Miss Aria."

"They'll be back soon. They are cruising Europe." Aria looks up before glancing at the images again. Her expression turns to one of perplexity. A particular painting strikes her as hauntingly familiar, though she cannot place where she's seen it before. "Are these all the paintings you currently have on sale?"

"Yes, our inventory is meticulously current. That's a cornerstone of our success. Baroness Orczy, whom I had the pleasure of meeting at your parents' dinner yesterday, is expected to attend the gallery tomorrow morning. Thus, some paintings might go." He reaches out his hand to Aria, who returns the photograph with a faint smile. As she places them in his palm, she can't help but notice the rough, calloused texture of his palm.

"Have you been in England long, Lord Montgomery?" Aria asks. Lord Montgomery freezes, unaccustomed to being interrogated by someone so young.

"Several years now... May I ask why you're interested?"

Realizing her question might spark suspicion, Aria backs off. "Oh, it's just that my brother and I are also from the Americas. We haven't been here very long, so perhaps our families are acquainted."

His expression flickers briefly before he resettles into his characteristic charming smile. "It's been quite some time, and I'm afraid I don't recognize the name," he responds, guiding them towards the exit. "My daughter will return shortly. You may wait for her in the library."

The girls offer parting smiles and look around the room one final time before heading out. As they retrace their steps, Aria whispers to Mary Louise, "I never gave our supposed last name!"

Mary Louise gasps. "Do you think we should wait for Victoria? She might have information."

"She won't be of any help to us, and Liam and James are likely waiting. We've gathered enough here; it's time to visit our next suspect."

The girls scurry out, barely acknowledging the footman as they rush to find Liam and James.

"What have you found out?" Aria asks before she even reaches them.

"The servants have shared quite a bit," James says with a grin.

"They're a treasure trove of gossip!" Liam chimes in, leaving Aria with a hint of envy for not accompanying James. As they walk, the boys excitedly share their discoveries, causing the girls' excitement to grow with each new piece of information they learn.

"So, could Louisa be a suspect?" Aria says, momentarily forgetting she's speaking of Mary Louise's mother.

Mary Louise's shock is palpable. "How can you suggest that?"

"We can't remove any possibilities. It's just part of a thorough investigation," Aria says gently.

Mary Louise is speechless, prompting Liam to change the subject. "And what about your visit with the Montgomerys?"

"Nothing concrete, but some elements tickle my brain," Aria says as she contemplates the bustling street.

"Can you please tell us what makes your brain *tickle*, my dear Aria?" Liam teases her.

Ignoring his amusement, she replies, "Lord

Montgomery showed us photos of paintings for sale. One seemed familiar, yet I can't place it." Aria's thoughts drift. "And his hands were... odd."

"In what way?" Liam presses, wondering if Aria's imagination is running wild again.

"It's hard to describe... just a feeling," she insists as they approach Baroness Orczy's neighborhood.

A hushed stillness settles over the group as they navigate the bustling streets of London. The turn of the century brings a mix of modern cars and old-fashioned carriages weaving around each other. People rush chaotically while men in sharp suits sit on elevated chairs, waiting for their shoes to shine until they can see their own reflections. The class system is clear just by observing how everyone dresses. They all walk on the same sidewalks, but it's like they're in entirely different worlds, each sticking to the life they were born into.

Aria slows her pace as she spots a boy excitedly calling out the news from the front page of a newspaper. Her face winces as she looks at the paper, oddly familiar.

"Isn't it the same where you're from?" Mary Louise asks.

"Are you kidding? No way!" Liam bursts out, earning puzzled looks from Mary Louise and James. He clears his throat, searching for the correct description. "It's more modern, more... technological, and less..." He pauses, knitting his brows in thought.

"Graceful," Aria chimes in, her choice of words bringing happiness to Mary Louise.

Liam's response is cut short by Aria's nudge— now is not the time for debate. Mary Louise redirects their attention to a Victorian townhouse across the street.

This residence, in stark contrast to Lord Montgomery's, is distinctly humbler with its traditional brown brickwork. It's a three-story structure with *only* two windows per level.

Aria whirls around to look at Liam. "I have an idea! Why don't you go with Mary Louise this time, and I go with James?" she exclaims.

"You want to go deliver the milk? You?"

"Yes, why not? It's hard work I am guessing, so you earned the right to get a little rest."

"I do it all day and don't get to rest!" James chimes in.

Liam stares at her incredulously before smiling. "You want to hear all the gossip, that's why!" He points at her as he unmasks her true motive.

Aria crosses her arms over her chest, ready to defend her honor before bursting into laughter. "Okay… you got me!"

The group splits into their pairs. Aria follows James to the servants' quarters while Liam and Mary Louise make their way to the porch. Liam confidently plans to use his charming persona to gather any information from the baroness. Liam knocks aggressively on the door, excited to peek at life upstairs. Mary Louise clenches her teeth as she looks at him before reaching for a bell beside the doorway, sending a clear ringing sound into the home.

A man with striking green eyes and neatly styled blond hair opens the door. They are quickly welcomed into the modest interior of the house, reflecting its unpretentious exterior.

"The baroness is occupied with her writing. Please wait here while I seek her permission to admit you," the butler informs them before heading down the corridor. He halts suddenly, turning back with a questioning look. "May I inquire as to the purpose of your visit?"

Caught off-guard, Liam and Mary Louise exchange a quick, uncertain glance.

"We're here to ask her some advice about her work, sir," Liam responds with a smile.

The butler nods and retreats, soon returning with permission for them to meet the baroness. "Her Ladyship is entertaining a guest but will be with you shortly," he tells them, standing rigidly by the office door before opening it. As they enter, they hear a man say, "You might want to disappear for a while."

Their expressions shift from eager anticipation to shock as they come face to face with Dr. Watson, hat in hand, already prepared to leave.

CHAPTER 15
BELOW THE STAIRS

James finds it difficult to keep pace with Aria, whose enthusiasm for joining the servants' gossip meeting prevents her from noticing the burden of his cart. At the stairwell, she descends so rapidly that she nearly stumbles.

"Ahem," James interjects from above, a bottle in each hand.

Aria whirls around, her eyes widening. "Oh! I'm so sorry!" she exclaims, hurrying back to assist him.

"Remember your role, or we'll be unmasked," he warns her before handing her a bottle and rushing down the stairs. Aria follows him into a quiet vestibule.

They enter the modest kitchen, where a woman

is engrossed in *The Strand Magazine*, her face a parade of emotions.

James sets down the bottles with a grin, the cook not even acknowledging him.

"Mrs. Smith, I see you're caught up in your stories. But would you like the latest scoop?" he asks, his lips curling in a smile.

Her attention snaps to James, her expression lighting up. She inclines toward him. "I am all ears!"

Without delay, he spins a tale about a new Sherlock Holmes adventure. Mrs. Smith's jaw drops, the magazine tumbling from her hands.

"Are you serious?" she breathes.

"Absolutely. We just came from the Doyles' house," James assures her.

The cook stashes the bottles with excitement on her face. "Such a relief," she sighs, pausing when she notices Aria trying to blend in by the door. "And who's this?" she inquires.

"This is Aria," James begins, then hesitates, aware that milk delivery isn't typically a woman's work. "She's looking for a position. We're checking if any homes need a maid."

The cook eyes Aria skeptically. "That's quite an outfit you wear there," she says, pointing to the flashy red colors of her dress. "Seems you have other intentions...."

Aria's cheeks flush. "I... I found the dress in the trash, and I've worked as a maid before!" she stammers.

"We're fully staffed here," the cook says. "Try the Montgomerys; they're always hiring since no one seems to last long there."

Aria perks up. "Oh? Why is that?"

The cook begins to chop vegetables. "Word is, they're difficult people. His Lordship might be American, but he acts like an old British lord." She chuckles as she takes some vegetables from the pantry. "We normally don't have trouble in this house, at least not until today."

Aria shares a glance with James, who quickly asks the cook, "What happened?"

Mrs. Smith pauses, her knife hovering mid-air. She looks at them, baffled. "You're just coming back from the Doyles and haven't heard?" When Aria and James shake their heads, she adds, "The police are there! Sir Doyle left his family with only a poor note as an explanation." The news hits Aria and James like a bolt, leaving them momentarily stunned. The rumors James had been sharing had just become a startling reality.

"Are you sure?" James asks, his voice shaking.

"Absolutely! I'm always in the know. Dr. Watson himself told the baroness this morning. And you know what I think? Now that I learned Sir Doyle is about to revive his most lucrative character, I am sure he planned his exit alongside the return of Sherlock Holmes. It's not a secret that his wife's illness is driving him away. And with his new stories, he likely doesn't want her to get the fortune he will make," the cook speculates, her hands busy with her culinary tasks, oblivious to their shock.

"But why would the police be involved if he's just left?" Aria's tone is tinged with frustration by the cook's hasty conclusions.

Mrs. Smith looks up from her chopping. "Who knows? Perhaps he's taken something or trying to force her out."

Aria feels angry at the slander of a writer she admires. She's about to retort when James intervenes. "Thank you, Mrs. Smith. We should be off. See you tomorrow."

"Yes, but don't be late this time. There's a significant dinner in honor of the baroness's new book, and I need to start early."

James nods and quickly exits, tugging Aria along.

They leave in silence, their expressions betraying their inner turmoil.

Aria explodes once they're in the street. "She's having a dinner party tomorrow! Don't you get it? She's behind Doyle's disappearance! She wants no competition, especially now that she knows he is about to revive Sherlock Holmes, the greatest detective!"

"We can't be certain. Let's wait for the others and compare notes," James suggests, hoping their friends have found more reliable information.

$$\mathrm{Q}$$

SILENCE REIGNS in the baroness's office, broken only by the distant sounds of the street.

Baroness Orczy stands from her colossal chair behind her desk. "Mary Louise, I must say I'm surprised to see you here after what your father did." Mary Louise's expression reveals her bewilderment.

Dr. Watson steps forward, signaling the baroness to let him handle it. "What the Baroness wants to say is that after your father's departure this morning, perhaps you should be with your mother now, Mary Louise."

She gasps, wordless.

"What do you mean?" Liam interjects, making the two adults confused.

Dr. Watson adjusts his hat. "My apologies. I did not know you had not been notified. As soon as I learned about Arthur's unexpected departure, I came here to inform the baroness. Mary Louise, your father left your home never to return this morning. He left a message to explain his decision."

Liam's forehead creases as he listens to the news, while Mary Louise begins to sob, unable to control the avalanche of emotions falling on her.

"You're behind this!" Mary Louise accuses, anger coursing through her. Dr. Watson winces, the baroness looking on, baffled. "What have you done to my father?"

"How dare you suggest Dr. Watson or I had any hand in this? Your father left of his own accord," the baroness says, stepping next to Dr. Watson, who is motionless.

"It's your secret society! I'll uncover the truth about my father!" Mary Louise cries despite Liam's attempts to calm her.

Dr. Watson approaches, concern etched on his face. "Why would you think that?"

"This is absurd!" the baroness exclaims while Dr. Watson gestures for calm.

"I have been warned," Mary Louise says, meeting his gaze.

The baroness scoffs. "You should go home to your mother, or I'll call her to tell her."

With a loud sob, Mary Louise wrenches herself free from Liam's grip and bolts from the room, tears streaming down her face. She runs so fast that Liam only catches up to her outside, where James and Aria anxiously wait.

"What happened?" Aria asks, seeing Mary Louise's distress.

Liam quickly updates them, his expression darkening upon hearing their news. "The police? But if it was his own choice to leave, why involve them?"

"That's exactly what I said!" Aria exclaims.

"He didn't leave willingly! I'm certain!" Mary Louise says between two tears.

"We have to gather more information. They talked about a note he wrote. It should give us more clues," Liam says.

"Do you really think he left just like that?" Aria asks.

Liam exhales deeply. "I'm not sure, but it doesn't add up. You heard the threats he faced, and he seemed reluctant about Sherlock Holmes. Maybe he was forced to leave," Liam suggests, the others staring at him in shock. "We need to stay level-headed."

Aria's heart pounds as she declares, "There's only one way to know for certain—we must go back." They nod in agreement and start the return journey to the Doyle residence.

CHAPTER 16
THE POLICE AT WORK

S ilent tears stream down Mary Louise's face as she quickens her pace, the weight of unspoken thoughts heavy on her mind. The house looms ahead, but her attention is drawn to two magnificent horses standing in front. Their glossy black hides and perfect white hooves dazzle in the sunlight, a stark contrast to the sealed-off carriage they are connected to. Bold letters spelling "PATROL" are painted up the side, adding an air of urgency and danger to the scene.

"Mary Louise, wait!" Aria calls, racing to catch up. She grasps her arm to stop her. "We can't go in through the front door! Remember, we escaped."

"She's right," Liam says, arriving with James

close behind. "Your mother will ground us if she finds out!"

"I don't care! My dad has been kidnapped or..." Mary Louise's voice breaks, unable to say the word 'murdered.'

"It won't help your dad if we're locked inside the house! Your mom will know we snuck out the window," Aria argues.

"Maybe we can sneak in through the servants' entrance?" Liam suggests.

"I'll distract them while you go in," James offers.

Mary Louise stares at the house, which once had a pleasant feeling but now has an eerie atmosphere. She nods and trails behind the group.

James quickly looks around to ensure the path is free of anyone watching. He ducks down and walks towards the side of the house, with the others following him closely. He cautiously descends the stairs to the servants' hall before signaling the others to come. The layout is divided into three sections: the kitchen and servants' dining area on one side, the butler's office on the opposite side, and a lengthy hallway heading into the house.

James races to the kitchen, his announcement of the scoop of the year catching the servants' attention. Without delay, the maids gather the staff in the room.

"They definitely love the gossip!" Liam chuckles as they hear the house staff rushing past the door to the kitchen.

"Yes, but can you imagine working like that all day for so little? They need some sort of reward!" She steps back, startled, as a servant slams the door shut, muffling the sounds from inside instantly.

The trio stands in silence, straining their ears for any conversation from the other side of the wall. After a short pause, Aria suggests they should go in and slowly turns the doorknob and peeks her head through the opening. James's voice, loud and full of excitement, fills the kitchen, mingled with the servants' astonished reactions. He certainly has a talent for storytelling!

She signals Liam and Mary Louise and then slips inside, walking cautiously along the corridor. Feeling the dull thud of her boots against the cobblestone, she tiptoes instead. Their hearts pound as they hurry, the servants' shocked gasps echoing behind them.

They reach the staircase and bound up two steps at a time. They pause at the top, their heavy breathing echoing through the silence.

Aria gently eases the door open, peering into the empty vestibule. Her face is tense with anticipation as she enters, followed by Liam and Mary Louise. Suddenly, without warning, Aria rushes towards the staircase, her movements quick and fluid as she begins jumping from one step to the next. Liam and Mary Louise watch in astonishment before Aria returns to their side, a wide grin spreading across her face.

"What? We must look like we've just come from upstairs!" she insists.

The door behind Liam swings open abruptly, startling them. Clifford emerges, his expression even more strained than usual. His eyes widen at the sight of them, and his brow furrows.

"Clifford, is Mama here? I need to talk to her," Mary Louise blurts.

Wordlessly, Clifford steps aside and gestures toward the room he just left. Mary Louise rushes into the library, with Aria and Liam close behind. When they see Louisa standing there, clutching the doll Aria used for her trick, with two police officers and Nurse Penny looking at them contemptuously, they instantly freeze.

"Mama, we—"

"Don't speak," Louisa cuts her off sharply as she

rises, her gaze piercing. She turns to the officers. "Chief Brown, thank you for coming. I must attend to a personal matter now," she says, fixing her gaze on Mary Louise.

"We understand, Lady Doyle. We'll leave you," Chief Brown replies, nodding farewell before exiting with the constable.

Aria steps forward. "Wait!" she shouts, stunning the adults. "We might have information for your investigation."

The chief of police pauses and faces her, his look filled with skepticism. Aria shivers under his stern gaze. "We have what we need, and I doubt a child can contribute. Stick to games for your age, not adult matters," he says harshly.

Aria's fear morphs into defiance. "But I think—" Liam nudges her, sensing trouble brewing. Chief Brown gives her a wry smile and departs.

"Mama, I swear we—" Mary Louise starts, but her mother's sharp gesture silences her.

"Enough!" she bellows, then coughs violently. Mary Louise moves to help, but her mother waves her off, settling her cough. "I've been through enough this morning with your father gone and us left in this chaos—"

"He didn't abandon us!" Mary Louise protests, only to ignite her mother's anger further.

"You don't understand these things, Mary Louise. You act like you're grown, breaking the rules, hanging out with troublemakers," Louisa scolds, eyeing Aria and Liam with disdain. After a cough, she adds, "This ends now. Your father has left, and we're moving back to Undershaw. The chief of police just brought me the note your father sent to the police station to announce he will not return."

"He didn't write it!" Mary Louise exclaims, bewildered.

Louisa's breath quickens as she locks eyes with her daughter, then pulls a note from her pocket and hands it to Mary Louise. The girl gasps, covering her mouth as she reads. Aria and Liam lean in for a glance, but Louisa snatches it back. "There's nothing more to discuss. You'll stay locked in your room until we leave London," Louisa declares, ignoring her daughter's protests.

Aria steps up, her gaze steady on Louisa. "Lady Doyle, we have evidence—"

"Stop now! Why should I trust you after all the lies? I welcomed you into my home, and now I find out nobody even knows who you are or anything about your so-called nurse or parents," Louisa shouts before nodding to Nurse Penny. "She's seen through your charade. At least I have her to make me see the truth. Maybe you even stole something. Who knows who you are."

"They are my friends!" Mary Louise intervenes.

Louisa's body trembles as her rage grows. "Your so-called friends? Are they the ones telling you your father has been kidnapped or is in danger? Mary Louise, these people are not your real friends. Your father has left, and you must accept it."

Liam jumps in, his voice powerful. "We're trying to help, not cause trouble! Yes, we had to lie about who we are, but if you'd listen, maybe we could find your husband and go back home where we are not screamed at!" His outburst leaves Louisa and Nurse Penny in shock while Aria looks on with a mix of awe and pride.

But their plea falls on deaf ears. Soon, Aria and Liam are escorted out, the Doyle's residence door firmly shutting behind them. Standing on the porch, they exchange panicked glances. Their quest to help has led them to a dead end, ousted from the very place where they hoped to find answers.

CHAPTER 17

NOTHING IS MISSING

Aria and Liam stand quietly on the porch, watching the busy street before them. Aria sighs, pondering their next move.

"I'm sorry," Liam whispers, sneaking glances at Aria.

Her shoulders slump as she says, "It's okay."

Liam's face turns to surprise, shocked by Aria's calm, who he assumed would blame him. "This must have really upset you for you to react like this!"

"It's a setback, but I'm actually impressed you stood up for us!" She grins at him. Suddenly, her eyes catch something on the street and her face lights up. She grabs Liam's arm and tugs it, pointing to the police carriage. A group of officers stands guard, all dressed in navy uniforms with gleaming buttons, white gloves, and the typical Scotland Yard helmet. Whistles are attached to chains around their necks, and handcuffs hang from their belts.

"What is it?" Liam squints, trying to see what's caught Aria's attention.

"There!" Aria pulls him along. "It's James!" she cries, hurrying toward him. James is deep in conversation with the constable they saw in the living room earlier. His face brightens upon seeing the pair approaching. The constable frowns, his gaze hardening as he notices them.

A heavy silence envelops the group as they join James. He addresses the constable. "Thanks for your help, constable. I hope this problem gets sorted out soon!"

The constable nods and walks toward the police carriage. "Wait!" Aria's voice halts him. "Did you find anything unusual?" she asks boldly.

The constable squints at her. He's about to reply when Chief Brown bursts behind them, barking, "What are you still doing here? This case is closed, and if you don't leave, I'll have you arrested."

"Arrest us?" Liam's brow furrows. "But we're only thirteen!"

The policemen burst out laughing, making Liam even more confused. Chief Brown's face reddens as he moves closer to Liam, who steps back. "And why not?"

Liam stands still as James comes to his rescue. "Our apologies, we are leaving now. We are just worried about Lady Doyle."

The chief's expression softens as he turns to the boy. "It's merely a sad case of home abandonment, not a crime. You should head home and let the authorities handle this." He signals his officers to board the carriage.

The coachman commands the horses, and the carriage slowly moves away from the house, fading out of sight as the three watch silently.

Aria turns to Liam. "Just so you know, you can get arrested at thirteen here. They aren't indulgent with age in these times."

Liam's expression tightens. "Really?"

"Yes," confirms James.

Liam shakes his head. "Aria, sometimes I wonder why you are so passionate about history!"

"Remember, Liam," Aria says with a touch of defiance in her tone, "it's only thanks to the turbulence of the past that we can enjoy freedom today!"

Liam takes in her statement before dismissing it. Now is not the time for philosophical thoughts. He looks back at the departing police carriage. "That chief of police is..." he begins.

"Lying," James cuts in, drawing their attention.

"Did you find out something?" Aria asks.

"Indeed, I did. The man I spoke with said they searched through the house and didn't find anything missing," James smiles.

Aria's hand flies to her mouth. Liam stares, puzzled. "How does that help us?"

"Liam!" Aria grips his shoulder. "It means Sir Doyle didn't leave by choice. If he had, he would've taken his belongings." Liam's jaw drops in realization. Aria winces before turning to James. "Then why isn't this being treated as a kidnapping?"

"That's the enigma. The constable senses something's off, but the chief won't hear it. He claims Doyle's notes say he planned to leave, which, to him, means there's no case."

"We didn't get to read the note closely..." Aria trails off, trying to remember. "Surely, a note isn't enough to be so certain?"

"I bet it's his pride," Liam suggests. "He just wants to be right—or perhaps he's too lazy to investigate properly."

"Yes, but it's a famous author who has vanished!" Aria stresses.

Liam waves a dismissive hand. "He's just an author, Aria, not a world-changing figure."

Aria's face colors with annoyance. "Liam, you should realize that authors—"

"Hey, mates! We should get going unless we want to finish this debate behind bars." James nods towards the house where Clifford stands, arms folded sternly.

They sidestep to the opposite sidewalk, vanishing from view. They stand silently, watching people stream out of the park as dusk approaches.

Liam rubs his hands together and breathes on them for warmth. His expression turns to curiosity as he watches a man climb a ladder to light a street lamp and then move on to the next. "Is he lighting all of them?"

"Of course," Aria responds, watching the lamp-lighter. "How else would the streets be lit at night? Electricity isn't common yet."

Liam ponders the effort it takes to live without modern conveniences.

"What do we do now?" Aria says, her patience waning.

James's gaze doesn't stray from the house, waiting for a glimpse of Mary Louise. "She'll find a way to come out."

"I'm not so sure. Her mother was furious, and they said they'd lock her in. They might even secure her window. Now they know we can escape," Liam says.

"We can't just leave her!"

"For now, we might have to. We're not helping her father by standing here," Aria says. "And what do you suggest? Breaking in? With all their staff, we will be caught in no time!"

"Aria is right, I am afraid. We should find somewhere to stay for the night. It's too cold." Liam shivers, his outfit being far enough for the London weather.

James takes a deep breath. "You're probably right. Let's head to my place—my mother loves having visitors. It's time for you two to see how life is on the other side of London!" Aria and Liam exchange wary glances, having heard of all the dangers lurking in the city's more impoverished parts.

"We can't wait," Liam winces.

As they leave, their hearts are filled with hope of seeing Mary Louise again soon. Little do they know a carriage pulls up to the Doyle residence at that very moment.

CHAPTER 18
THE FORTUNE TELLER

M ary Louise bites her nails as she paces
her room. Memories of the confronta-
tion with her mother replay in her
mind. Why is she so sure that her father aban-
doned them? The note supposedly from him had
strange handwriting, and he hadn't taken any
possessions, not even his latest Sherlock Holmes
manuscript.

The suspicion that Liam was right about her
mother's involvement sends shivers down her
spine. She tries the window again, but it's still firmly
locked. Someone must have come to lock it when
they were out. She spins around as her bedroom
door opens. A young maid, not much older than
herself, steps in with a tray.

"Your dinner, Miss Mary Louise," she says, setting the tray on the desk.

"Thanks, Daisy," Mary Louise replies, managing a smile. The maid curtsies and starts to leave when Mary Louise calls, "Daisy, wait!"

"Yes, miss?"

"I'm... concerned about my mother."

Daisy offers a look of understanding. "It must be hard...."

Tears suddenly spill from Mary Louise's eyes, and she covers her face. Daisy rushes to embrace her. "She will be fine, Miss Mary Louise. Your mother has company right now."

Mary Louise looks up, intrigued. "What do you mean?"

Daisy hesitates, then whispers, "Baroness Orczy is with her. She came to retrieve a manuscript your father was holding for her."

The mention of Baroness Orczy halts Mary Louise's tears, her mind racing. "Baroness Orczy? Really?"

"Yes, I had to fetch the manuscript for her."

Clifford's voice from downstairs, calling for Daisy, cuts their exchange short. The maid curtsies again and hurries out, leaving Mary Louise with a new puzzle piece.

She retrieves a hairpin from her dressing table and angrily attacks the window lock. Her hands are slick with sweat as she jiggles the pin, her heart pounding. Frustration mounts until she hears a click; the lock springs open. She wastes no time, slipping out the window into the cool night.

Rushing through the garden to the street, with the night darkening her path, she violently collides with someone. When she looks up, she refrains a cry as she sees the red-haired man who's been lingering nearby these past few days. His gaze is severe as he smirks at her. "Going somewhere?" he taunts.

Mary Louise, frozen with fear, can't respond. The man leads her back to the house, her chance of escape slipping away.

🔍

ARIA AND LIAM TRUDGE behind James, their bodies turning red from the piercing cold. Finally, James stops at a bus stop, bringing a glimmer of hope to their tired faces. "Just one ride away," he assures them with a faint smile. In no time, a double-decker omnibus comes into view, drawn by majestic horses and driven by a coachman perched on the front seat. The upper deck is open to the outside and packed with passengers, while windows shelter the lower deck. A passenger steps down to let them board. Aria rushes up the stairs to the upper deck so quickly she nearly topples backward, saved only by Liam's quick reflexes. They find seats, blending in with the crowd. Watching them, no one would believe they're embroiled in one of the cases that will defy London chronicles for years to come.

As they travel, the scenery gradually shifts from grand townhouses to more humble neighborhoods. Dim gas lamps cast a soft glow on narrow alleys, revealing modest homes and the occasional flutter of laundry above. The faint glimmer of rain can still be seen on the cobblestones, adding to the eerie feel of the area. When the bus reaches Hoxton, James gestures for them to disembark. Aria braces herself, the memory of grand parties fading.

"Cheer up, Aria! You'll get used to it!" Liam teases as he hops off the bus.

"And you'll be the first to miss our usual comforts," Aria shoots back, looking to her new surroundings.

"Remember, I've braved tougher spots than this on our travels!" Liam grins.

"Let's not waste time here." James walks fast, making Aria and Liam run to keep pace with him.

"Do you have any brothers or sisters?" Aria asks, trying to counter her fear with conversation.

"No... I mean, I had a sister, but she died of smallpox when she was six."

"I am so sorry," Liam says. "So, you live with your mother and father?"

"Only my mother for now. My father is a sailor who spends much time at sea."

"He must have so many fascinating stories of adventure to tell you!" Aria beams.

"Yes and no. He is not often with us, but that pays well, so my mother is happy," James says as he turns into a shadowy alley.

With only the moon for light, their hearts race. A man appears from a doorway, causing Liam to jump with surprise. His face is smudged with black marks as if he has been through a chimney. He stares at the boy before continuing on his way, cigarette in hand.

"Got a bit of a fright, did we, my dear Liam?" Aria teases, noting his pale face.

Liam stays silent, still shaking from the encounter. James leads them into a house, its entrance obscured by laundry hanging on a clothesline. A dim light emanates from within, casting eerie shadows along the old wooden walls of the corridor. The air is musty and heavy and closed doors line the path to a narrow staircase ahead.

As they walk toward the stairs, a woman bursts from a doorway, seizing Aria's arm. Aria trembles, facing the woman, whose impressive presence is accentuated by her curly hair cascading to her waist. The woman's intense brown eyes peer into Aria's soul as she speaks cryptically. "To save a king, you must unveil the golden disguise of the ones close to him."

Aria's breath catches, and the woman releases her arm, a smile dawning on her face. Liam presses against the wall for support and fights to steady his shaking legs.

"Anne, you'll scare our guests away!" James

shouts from the stairs. The woman smiles at him and retreats to her room without a word.

Aria and Liam hurry up the stairs. "Who was that?" Aria asks, rushing up.

"She's a fortune teller," James responds, continuing past floors where the weary inhabitants move about.

"A fortune teller?" Aria echoes, surprised.

"Does this mean that now we're to save a king too?" Liam asks, exasperated.

James shrugs. "I don't know, but King Edward II came into power recently, and I don't think many people like him! Hard to fill his mother's shoes."

As they reach a landing, Liam leans into Aria, "Who was his mother?"

"Queen Victoria. She is still considered in our time as one of the greatest English monarchs," Aria whispers. Seeing the fearful look on her best friend's face, she tries to lighten the mood with a joke. "Maybe that's just a hint of our next mission!"

"That's supposed to make me feel better? Kings or any powerful people are always the worst to deal with..." Aria keeps silent, sharing his sentiment. James waves them in, bringing them back to reality. There is no time to think about kings when they have the life of the greatest author in their hands.

CHAPTER 19
THE SUSPECTS LIST

They enter James's modest living space, where a fire in the chimney offers warmth. The room is sparsely furnished, with only a wooden table and four chairs arranged in the center. A couple of plain armchairs are placed around the fire. The tapestry on the wall shows signs of wear. In one corner, laundry hangs by the fireplace, drying in the warmth.

"Mama!" James calls as he heads for an adjacent room, leaving Aria and Liam behind.

A warm voice responds, "My son!" A woman with a welcoming smile takes James's face in her hands and kisses his cheek.

James hands her some coins. "Earned this today. Also, I've brought a couple of friends."

The woman, entering the living room, wears a long red-and-white checkered dress that flows nearly to the floor. As she steps in, she tidies her thick shawl around her shoulders. Her fiery red hair and features mirror James's. "Welcome. I'm Mrs. Evans," she says, addressing Aria and Liam, who hesitate on the landing. "Please, come in and sit down!"

"Thank you," Aria says softly, settling into an armchair. Mrs. Evans drapes a blanket over her. "You look chilled in that thin dress," she notes with a caring smile. As she turns to Liam, her brows furrow when she sees the ill-fitting state of his clothes.

"It's a long story," Liam says, catching her inquisitive look.

"Hand it over. I'll mend it," Mrs. Evans offers promptly.

Liam, grateful, starts to remove his jacket as Mrs. Evans retrieves her sewing kit and disappears into the nearby room.

Once alone, James takes a chair and settles by the fire in front of them. Aria relaxes, mesmerized by the flickering flames. "This mystery is far more difficult than any we've faced!"

"Don't tell me! I'm still wondering if Doyle left on his own..." Liam replies, under the confused gazes of the other two. "Look, I know it seems unlikely, but we can't rule out every possibility until we figure it out."

"Let's review what we've found out," Aria says with determination before shifting to dismay. "I left our notes back in Mary Louise's room." She sighs as she keeps patting her pocket.

Liam grins, pulling out his phone. "Good thing I have my notes right here," he boasts, teasing Aria.

Aria extends her hand for the phone, but Liam moves away faster. "Let's get to it, then," he says, thumbs poised to type.

"Fine, but make sure you get it all down," Aria says, earning an eye roll from Liam. "We'll review each suspect, just like Sherlock would," she adds excitedly.

"Starting with Louisa Doyle," Liam says, feeling the weight of their stares. "Can we just focus? We need to consider every angle to solve this."

"Alright, Louisa Doyle," Aria says. "She had fought with Doyle about his writing the night before he vanished, dismissed the warning Mary Louise received, but trusts the note supposedly written by her husband that was sent to the police."

"And despite the police noticing that Doyle's personal items weren't taken, she still believes he left," James adds.

"But she didn't leave the house that morning," Aria counters, puzzled.

Liam nods. "She could have an accomplice. What about Mr. Clifford?"

"Maybe. He did leave the house! We need a motive. There's always one," Aria muses.

James intervenes. "Money. It often drives people to get rid of their spouses."

Aria and Liam nod in agreement, finding this explanation credible.

Liam types this down. "Next is Baroness Orczy. Her motive is simple: she doesn't want Doyle to continue writing and overshadow her. "

Aria frowns. "But she only found out he was writing a detective novel again after the warning to Mary Louise."

"Perhaps she's working with Dr. Watson. Doyle might have shared his plans with Watson." Liam suggests.

"That makes sense!" Aria exclaims. "Don't you remember? At dinner, Watson reacted oddly when Doyle announced he'd bring back Sherlock Holmes. He probably wanted Doyle to give up writing," she recalls vividly.

Liam's expression changes as he remembers the moment. "You're right!"

"I tend to always be, my dear Liam," Aria smirks.

Liam ignores her comment. "That will explain the blackmail. As he did not obey, they stopped him by force. And Watson's words to the baroness about disappearing for a while... It shows they are working together!"

"But why would Watson want to stop Doyle from writing the next Sherlock Holmes?" James interjects, adding a new layer to their speculations.

Liam rubs his temples, the complexity of their theories making his head spin.

Aria's eyes gleam with conviction. "It could be about the Freemasons! When the last Sherlock Holmes came out, he was still part of this society. Doyle's novels often implicate powerful figures, and maybe they fear he'll expose secrets now that he's left the order. Writers hide truths in their fiction; everybody knows that," she explains with confidence.

"That could be it," James acknowledges, and Liam nods in agreement.

"Write that down. Now, onto Lord and Lady Montgomery," Aria says, shifting gears. "He sold Doyle paintings and has money troubles. Could it be about money?"

Liam stares into space, deep in thought. "But would financial problems drive someone to make a person vanish? That's a little bit extreme."

"People do drastic things when desperate," James says. "A ransom, perhaps?"

"We may need to check that tomorrow. It could also have to do with Doyle's novel. Contrary to the others, he knew he was writing the next one, as he mentioned it during his speech," Aria says.

Liam contorts his lips. "Maybe he wants to..." He stops, squeezing his eyes to try to see another motive.

Aria abruptly stands, startling the other two. "How could I have forgotten!" She taps her head in disbelief. "Remember when I told you one of the photographs caught my attention, but I couldn't remember how?" They nod, perplexed. "Now I know why! It is the exact same painting we saw in the Doyle's house!"

Liam looks at her, perplexed. "It might only be a mistake."

"But he was sure about his inventory's accuracy," Aria insists.

Liam dismisses it with a wave. "Probably just pride."

"Or maybe that's his wife. We should consider everyone!" James chimes in.

Aria's face lights up as she recalls her encounter with Lady Montgomery. "She did look a little bit fake when she talked to Mary Louise. Maybe she is having an affair with Doyle and is just waiting to flee as well?"

Their brainstorming is cut short by loud knocks on the door. They freeze, turning their attention toward the sound.

CHAPTER 20
ANY HELP IS WELCOMED

The group remains frozen, hands shaking, as the loud pounding on the door intensifies.

"Are you expecting someone?" Aria whispers at last.

"No..." James replies, standing with trembling legs.

"Don't!" Liam cuts in. "Maybe we've been followed. Now, everyone knows we're snooping around, and from what you've told me about the Freemasons, I'd rather not face them!"

"But what if it's Mary Louise?" James counters, moving toward the door. Suddenly, his mother bursts into the living room, her brow furrowed.

"Why won't you answer?" she demands as the knocking continues.

"Mama, no!" James shouts just as Mrs. Evans opens the door.

James' heart leaps with relief when he sees Anne standing in the doorway, her lips curled into a playful smirk.

"Anne, how lovely to see you!" Mrs. Evans greets her. "What brings you here?"

"Good evening, Mrs. Evans. I wanted to talk with James and his friends," Anne says, nodding at Aria and Liam, who sit motionless.

"Please, come in. Don't just stand there," Mrs. Evans insists, ushering her in with delight. Suddenly, she exclaims, "Oh! I almost forgot. I need to pick up a dress from my sister," she said, scurrying to the next room. After a few moments, she comes back and hands Liam a jacket. "This should fit you well, dear." Liam stands and slips on the jacket that suits him perfectly. He notices how, finally, the fabric follows his movements as he swings his arms around. A grateful smile spreads across his face. "Thank you, Mrs. Evans."

"It's nothing," she responds, draping a wool shawl around her shoulders. "I'll be out for a bit.

There are sandwiches in the kitchen for you." James kisses her cheek and closes the door after her.

Anne scrutinizes the group with a black canvas bag tightly clasped to her chest. "I hope I'm not bothering you, but I had to come. They won't leave me alone until I do."

Liam frowns. "Who?"

"The spirits," Anne says, as if explaining the rain.

Liam's eyes widen before he bursts into laughter. "Spirits? That's a good one!"

Aria fixes her gaze on Liam. "I don't think she's making it up, Liam," she says, and his laughter fades.

"I am not and have brought something." Anne reaches into her bag and extracts a mysterious object, placing it carefully on the table. Aria and Liam gather around James as he examines the curious object. It's a smooth, wooden board adorned with the alphabet in two arching rows, numbers from zero to nine, and "yes" and "no" at its corners. Anne takes out a small, heart-shaped planchette with a clear window, perfectly designed to fit snugly in one's hand.

"What's this?" Liam asks, a quiver in his voice.

Aria's eyes widen. "That's a Ouija board, isn't

it?" Anne confirms with a nod. James steps back, shaking.

"So, what does it do?" Liam asks, confused by Aria and James' differing reactions.

Anne sits down at the table. "I use this to talk to spirits when I need clear answers. Please, join me."

"I'm not sure about this," James stammers from a distance, looking as pale as a ghost.

Aria, eager with anticipation, sits next to Anne. "Come on, guys! This might really help us."

Liam hesitates, his gaze fixed on the board. "I'm not certain either. What if we stir up something evil?"

"Spirits are friendly." Aria laughs off his concern.

Liam's eyebrows arch skeptically. "Really? Did you get that from one of your books? You've never seen a ghost. How would you know?"

"You're right, I haven't," Aria admits. "But we won't find out unless we try! Don't be scared!"

Liam reluctantly settles into his seat, not wanting to give Aria the satisfaction of calling him out for backing out.

Anne turns to James. "There's nothing to be afraid of. I'm here."

James reluctantly moves to the table, beads of

sweat on his face. He sits while Anne places candles around the board. Liam takes deep breaths to settle his racing heart while Aria fidgets in her seat, barely containing her excitement.

With the final candle lit, Anne's gaze sweeps over the group, adding to the air of mystery. "I hear you're searching for that famous author who vanished."

"How did you know?" Liam's voice betrays his alarm.

"The spirits told you?" Aria leans in, her curiosity piqued.

"Yes, they've shared quite a bit about you two."

Liam swallows hard, his logical mind grappling with the situation.

"What have they said?" Aria comes in closer, prompting Anne to lean back.

"That's not what we should be asking now," Anne cuts. She places the planchette at the board's center. "Now, put a finger on this," she instructs, showing them how. Aria's finger lands so quickly that the planchette skids toward James across from her.

James, breathing hard, hesitantly obeys. Anne gives an encouraging nod from across Liam, who reluctantly joins in, muttering, "Nothing's going to happen. There are no such things as spirits."

"That's not what you said a minute ago, Liam!" Aria teases, rolling her eyes at him.

Anne, undistracted by their exchange, closes her eyes and breathes deeply. The others watch, puzzled by her concentration. Time slips by without any sign, and Aria begins to fidget impatiently. Liam's skepticism seems to return, reassured by the lack of supernatural events.

With another deep breath, Anne calls out, "Spirits, we seek your guidance to find answers." The silence that follows begins casting doubt, even in Aria.

Anne continues her chant, but nothing happens. Liam shakes his head in disbelief. "I thought so," he says but stops abruptly as the candle flames flicker wildly. He checks the window; it's shut tight. As Anne speaks again, the fireplace goes dark, startling them. Liam's fear is as swift to return as the extinguished flames. Aria's skin prickles with goosebumps as she watches the board intently.

"Now that you've joined us," Anne says as a draft sweeps through the room. "Can you tell us if Sir Conan Doyle is still alive?"

They all hold their breath as the room's air seems to stir. Suddenly, the planchette jerks toward the word "yes," making them all gasp in shock.

Unmoved, Anne thanks the spirits. "What can you tell us about those threatening him?"

The air around them becomes still and heavy. The candle flames flicker higher, prompting the group to take an involuntary lean back. Aria's enthusiasm fades into terror, her body shaking. The planchette starts to move under their fingers, spelling out "I-M-P-O-S-T-E-R."

"Liam, stop pushing it!" Aria protests, her voice tight with fear.

"I'm not doing anything!" Liam protests.

As they argue, the planchette stills and the room calms. Flames shoot up in the fireplace, giving them all a start. They sit silently, the word "imposter" echoing in their minds.

Anne is the first to remove her hand, and the others quickly follow. She smiles faintly, repacking the board. "You have your answer," she says as she stands up. "My work here is done." She leaves the others staring after her, motionless, the clue "imposter" hanging heavily in the air.

Q

Mary Louise hesitates briefly before confidently leading the way into the vestibule, the red-haired man following close behind. Lady Doyle and Baroness Orczy pause their conversation as they emerge from the library and notice their arrival.

"Mary Louise!" her mother cries, a mix of shock and dismay in her voice. "How did you..."

The man addresses Lady Doyle. "I found your

daughter alone outside, Lady Doyle. It's unsafe for her to be alone in London at this hour."

Regaining her poise, Louisa thanks him. She avoids Mary Louise's gaze as she orders her to go to her room. "I'll be coming to check on you soon so we can go over everything."

Mary Louise rushes upstairs, her heart racing. Reaching the first landing, she pauses to eavesdrop on the conversation below.

"Thank you for your support, Baroness. This ordeal has been overwhelming." Her mother's voice trembles.

"These situations are always challenging, particularly with public attention," replies the Baroness.

"My Lady, a call for you," Clifford announces.

"I'll be right there," Louisa responds. "And Mr. Parker, I'm grateful for your help this morning and now with my daughter. My apologies for the inconvenience."

Mary Louise's expression changes as she remembers the man coming in that morning. What kind of help was he supposed to provide?

"It's no trouble. Remember, we're always here to help."

Footsteps and the sound of a door echo up to Mary Louise. Then, nothing. She stealthily descends the stairs to get a better glimpse of what is happening. She notices the baroness in a heated discussion with Mr. Parker before the door. As she takes a few more steps downward, their words become clearer and clearer.

"...Scotland Yard. You must leave London soon, Baroness," Mr. Parker urges.

"I will, after one last thing is settled."

Mary Louise jumps back in panic as Clifford appears. She quickly runs upstairs to escape the situation. There's no doubt left in her mind—the baroness and the Freemasons are involved in her father's disappearance. She storms into her room, a whirlwind of emotion, and collapses at her desk. Rage builds within her as she contemplates her father's trust in those now betraying him.

She takes Aria's note and writes down all the new evidence they have gathered today to calm her nerves. As she looks at the complete list, her mother storms into her room, startling her startle. She quickly turns the paper down and walks to her bed.

Louisa stands in the doorway before joining her daughter on her bed. "Mary Louise, darling, what has gotten into you?" She asks as she caresses her hair.

"Mama, Papa is in danger, and you don't seem to believe me. We went to investigate today, and—"

"You what?" Louisa asks, standing. "Listen, I no longer want you to see those two kids. They have clearly had a bad influence on you."

"Ma—"

"Enough! This has gone too far. I don't even want to discuss it anymore."

Mary Louise turns her back, sobbing in her cushion as her mother leaves. When she hears the door closing, she turns back, her eyes puffy.

Her mother is oblivious to the truth unfolding before her. She weighs her options and concludes she must either convince her mother to help her or escape once more, hoping to reunite with Aria, Liam, and James.

Walking back to the window from where she had previously made her daring escape, she shoves it open farther and looks out cautiously. Noticing two men watching her, she gasps and starts to cry, burdened by the truth with no way of acting on it.

CHAPTER 21
BYE, BYE LONDON!

L iam trembles uncontrollably, rooted to the spot with fear. A figure with a menacing aura and wearing a black cloak strides toward him. The man's face is obscured by a mask that reveals only his mocking brown eyes. Liam's legs refuse to move, anchored in place. Sweat courses down his face as the man draws closer, soon to be upon him.

The masked man reaches up to reveal his identity. Liam squints, trying to make out the face, but his vision blurs with the sting of sweat in his eyes.

"Liam," a voice calls, jostling his arm. His vision is clouded. "LIAM!" His eyes snap open to find Aria peering down at him. Glancing around wildly, he sees James and his mother, their faces etched with concern.

"Come on, Liam, wake up! We have things to do," Aria says.

Liam winces as he rises from the cold, hard floor and feels a sharp pain in his back. His breathing steadies quickly as he wipes away the sweat from his forehead. "I had a nightmare," he murmurs, taking James's hand to stand up.

"We realized that. You kept screaming, 'imposter!' Seems like someone had a little fright," Aria teases, moving to help Mrs. Evans clear away the breakfast remains. "Sorry, but we ate without you. It's nearly nine, and we have a busy day ahead."

The echo of the previous night's Ouija board session lingers with Liam.

"Are you working today with James?" Mrs. Evans inquires.

After sharing a glance with James, Aria responds, "Yes, and in fact, we should have left already."

Hustling Liam along, Aria and James exit swiftly. Mrs. Evans hands Liam some bread, which he accepts with a muted thanks, still dazed.

"Who could be an impostor?" Aria wonders as

they descend the stairs, finally free from James' mother's earshot.

"It feels like everyone is," James responds.

As they leave the house, Aria halts suddenly, spinning to face them. "I've got it!" she exclaims, startling a nearby dog into barking.

"Could you lower your voice? My head is pounding," Liam pleads, massaging his temples.

Aria, undeterred, chides him, "Snap out of it, Liam. We don't have time to waste!" She dives back into their discussion. "The baroness! She must be the impostor. Perhaps she's not even a real author!"

James furrows his brow. "But why target Doyle?"

"To steal his manuscripts, of course!"

Liam scowls. "But how can she accomplish that if she kills him?" Aria exhales, her mind clouded by all the evidence presented. "It's possible Lord Montgomery is a fake art dealer. At this point, anyone could be an imposter," Liam adds, his voice heavy with despair as he cannot perceive any way out of the situation.

"We need to check what the police have as information," James says, urging them to keep moving.

"That's a great idea! Let's visit Scotland Yard and talk to the officers who were at Doyle's place yesterday," proposes Aria.

"Scotland Yard?" Liam echoes.

"Yes, the British police," Aria responds matter-of-factly.

Liam sighs. "And what do we tell them? That we're from the future and know something's happened to Doyle?"

Aria smiles. "I'm glad you're finally seeing Doyle didn't vanish on his own."

Liam brushes off the remark. "We'll have to find out from the police ourselves. They won't be happy to see us after yesterday."

Aria halts them. "Let's go in, and while one of us distracts the policemen, the others search."

Liam and James exchange a glance, surprised but agreeing, and they set off toward the wealthier parts of the city.

$$Q$$

MARY LOUISE, exhausted and on edge from lack of rest, gnaws at her nails, trying to make sense of the events that had happened the day before. The thought of her father, potentially still alive and being betrayed by those closest to him, causes a chill to run down her back. Liam's words about her mother's involvement reverberate in her mind.

She had spent the entire night attempting to dispute her suspicions, which only strengthened them. Her mother's unwavering faith in the supposed note from her father, the presence of his things still around the house and her mother's refusal to accept her warning all caused a deeper worry.

Frustrated, she charges at the window, attacking the newly installed lock with full force. Tears running down her face, she smashes at the panels with despair.

The sound of furniture being moved brings her out of her rage. She turns towards the door, which abruptly swings open.

Nurse Penny comes in with Daisy in tow, pulling a heavy trunk. Nurse Penny starts packing the girl's clothes without a word to Mary Louise.

"What are you doing? What's happening?" Mary Louise's voice quavers with her tears.

"You are going back to Undershaw," her nanny retorts bluntly.

Mary Louise's eyes widen in dismay and find a silent ally in Daisy's compassionate look.

"I won't go back! I need to find my father!" Mary Louise shouts, bolting from the nursery. She dashes down to the vestibule where her mother, already in her coat, awaits.

"Mary Louise, great, you're ready. We must leave now," Louisa announces, slipping on her gloves.

Mary Louise halts mid-descent as two men brush past her with the trunk.

"I'm not leaving without Father," she insists, her voice shaking.

Louisa's expression softens momentarily as she steps closer. "We must go, Mary Louise. We cannot stay here." She reaches for her daughter, who wrenches her hand away. Louisa's brief tenderness disappears. "You'll come, willingly or not. We can't delay."

At a nod from her mother, Mr. Clifford approaches to usher Mary Louise forward. Towering over her, he escorts her outside.

A carriage awaits, its back laden with trunks. The coachman holds the door as Louisa climbs in, Mary Louise trailing behind, her tears unabated.

Nurse Penny hastens to the carriage, sitting across from them. The coachman sets the horses in motion. Tears blur Mary Louise's last glimpse of her London home.

CHAPTER 22

SCOTLAND YARD

J ames, Aria, and Liam reach the Scotland Yard station. The outside of the building is tranquil and deserted.

"Let's rehearse one last time," Aria says, turning to James and Liam. "I run inside and inform them that my dog has been stolen. While the officer comes to help me, you two go inside and search the files."

"Let's hope the files aren't hidden or in a back room," Liam says under his breath, his face tense from such a shaky plan.

"They should be near the front desk, where they keep all the investigation records," James reassures. "I just hope they believe Aria and try to help her."

"Don't worry about that!" Aria beams, turning

back to the entrance. Surveying the bustling road, she times her move carefully. In this era, pedestrian crossings are few and far between, making any attempt to cross quite the adventure. Aria urgently gestures for them to hurry as they dodge a passing carriage. Together, they dash across the chaotic street, Liam narrowly avoiding a horseback rider.

Safely arriving on the sidewalk, Aria practices exaggerated mouth movements, prompting a puzzled glance from James. "She's getting into character," Liam explains with a wry grin.

"Here we go!" Aria smiles before adopting a look of sheer panic. She rushes toward the station doors, flailing dramatically, while the boys suppress their laughter.

She bursts into Scotland Yard, causing a commotion. The lone policeman at the desk jumps to his feet, baffled. "Thief! Thief!" Aria shrieks, her voice shrill. "Hurry, they've taken my dog!" Her frantic gestures pull the policeman into a frenzy, and he hurries after her, leaving the front desk unattended. Aria rushes outside with the police officer close behind, waving her arms wildly, garnering strange stares from passersby.

James and Liam slip inside amidst the chaos.

"I'll keep watch. You search," James tells Liam in a hushed tone.

"It'd be better if you checked the files—you know this place," Liam counters.

James's face falls. "I... I can't read," he confesses, leaving Liam taken aback. "Quick, before Aria can't distract them any longer!"

Liam darts behind the counter, where a daunting array of papers awaits him. He flicks through them rapidly, pausing only briefly on each. The reports should be more detailed for police documents. Usually, one or two sentences with no concrete evidence. Beneath a pile, he finds an open book with neatly organized columns. Names, dates, complaints, and notes from the investigators are all logged. A genuine lead at last, he thinks, grinning.

James peeks in. "Find anything? Aria won't keep them distracted for long!"

As Liam hurries through the entries, a report on a stolen goat makes him chuckle.

"What's funny?" James asks from the doorway.

"Nothing, just reading," Liam says, snapping back to the registry. His heart skips a beat when he spots Doyle's name, the entry merely citing "abandonment of home, nothing unusual found in the house." His forehead creases as he recalls the policeman's words to James. He starts to cover the book with the loose sheet when a surname jumps out. He looks at yesterday's date and finds that Lord Montgomery has submitted an accusation of blackmail. He stifles a gasp.

James runs to the counter to find out what Liam saw when an officer enters, accompanied by Aria, shouting injustice. She caught eye with them, and she quickly seizes the officer's arms to spin him towards her.

"Why won't you chase down the thief?" Aria says, drawing the officer's exasperation.

"A whole patrol for a dog, Miss Aria?" the officer replies, just as Liam slips out beside James.

"Why not?" Aria persists, testing his patience.

The officer explains the limitations of police resources, but Aria cuts him off as she spots Liam and James walking away from the desk. She feigns relief, but her act is short-lived as the officer quickly turns and sees the boys as well.

"What are you two doing here? Don't tell me your dog has been stolen, too," he says, mopping his brow.

Liam grins. "No, no dog here," he quips, lips pressed in a tight smile.

The officer scrutinizes Liam with suspicion. James says, "We came to file a complaint, but it looks like you're busy. We'll come back later."

Still recovering from Aria's performance, the officer sighs with relief and retreats to his desk. James, Liam, and Aria head towards the door, but their exit is interrupted by a sudden arrival.

Aria's heart sinks as Dr. Watson stands before them, his gaze locked onto theirs.

An awkward silence hangs in the air until Dr. Watson steps forward, removing his hat. "Good day to you three," he greets.

The officer, noticing the esteemed doctor, rises with a perplexed look. "Do you know them?"

Dr. Watson stays silent as he walks to the back of the station, announcing his intent to see the police chief.

"Yes, sir," the officer responds, showing him the way. He turns to the trio. "You three—"

But they're already out the door. The officer considers following them but decides against it. They have drained all his energy. He walks back to his desk, collapsing into his chair. His eyes catch the open book. Why were they here? After a sigh, he closes down the book. It's too late for pursuit. However, he'll need to alert the chief as soon as his meeting is over.

HAVING PUT distance between themselves and Scotland Yard, James, Aria, and Liam slow down, panting.

"Lord Montgomery's being blackmailed," Liam reveals, doubled over.

"Really?" James asks, astonished.

Aria pushes her damp hair back. "Are you certain?"

Liam nods. "But there was no other information. Their records are poor—no detail. Even for Doyle's disappearance, there was nothing about their investigation at the house. Believe me when I say they are certainly not master detectives!"

"If Montgomery's being blackmailed, he's in danger! We have to help him!" James cut in. "We need to head over to his house and warn him."

"No, he's probably at his art gallery right now," Aria says. "He mentioned yesterday that Baroness Orczy was coming by today to review his paintings."

Liam's eyes widen, and his mouth hangs agape. "We need to act quickly. If Lord Montgomery is not behind all this, it must be either Baroness Orczy or Dr. Watson!"

"And she is going there as we speak! Maybe Dr. Watson has gone to the station to occupy the chief while she carries out the criminal act!" Aria cries.

"Or worse: maybe they're trying to pin it on him!" Liam chimes in.

"I don't know, but we must act quickly!" James declares, setting off for the gallery. They run as they know every second counts.

CHAPTER 23

THE MISSING CLUE

Mary Louise sniffles, tears of anger and sadness mixing in her eyes. Her mother takes her hand, amplifying the young girl's despair. Nurse Penny looks at the carriage ceiling, allergic to any overflow of emotion.

"Mary Louise, look at me," Louisa says tenderly. "I know it's hard for you to accept, but we must return to Undershaw. It's no longer safe, I mean possible, for us to stay in London." Louisa turns away from Mary Louise, who is staring at her wide-eyed.

"You said safe? So, you also know Papa didn't leave alone?" she asks in a daze.

Louisa looks out the window of the carriage.

"There's no point discussing it; your father won't return." A single tear runs down her cheek.

Mary Louise grabs her arm, forcing her to look. "What do you mean by that? Do you know something I don't?" Her mother looks at her in silence, breathing heavily. "Mama, I know the Freemasons are behind all this. You have to believe me! We can still save Papa." When Nurse Penny hears these outlandish conspiracy theories, she cries out in shock. At the same time, Louisa's sarcastic laughter catches Mary Louise off guard.

"My dear, that's why kids should not mingle with adult matters. The Freemasons have nothing to do with your father's disappearance. On the contrary, they alerted me to the danger looming over us. And why would they harm your father?"

Mary Louise is taken aback. "What do you mean? Papa left them. Of course, they'd be mad at him and want to get revenge. Especially now that he is about to bring back Sherlock Holmes! They're probably worried about the things he'll write."

Louisa smiles at her. "Your father has already announced his return to their ranks."

This news hits Mary Louise like a bomb. It's the piece of information that turns their whole theory upside down. How was it possible she had no idea?

Thoughts of Aria, Liam, and James cross her mind
—the ones dealing with this situation without being
aware of this crucial information. She must find
them; they're undoubtedly in danger!

As their coach stops at a crossroads, Mary Louise
glances at her mother. "I'm sorry, Mama!" Stunned,
her mother watches as her daughter leaps from the
carriage just in time to avoid being hit by one of the
new speeding automobiles. Louisa shuts her eyes, too
startled to speak. When she regains her composure
enough to call out after Mary Louise, she finds the
street has already swallowed her daughter into its
chaotic hustle.

JAMES GUIDES ARIA and Liam through the bustling
streets between Scotland Yard and the wealthy area
where the Doyles live. The broad sidewalk is
crowded with people rushing to buy the newest
French fashions. It's a challenging run, avoiding the
umbrellas that dance above women's heads and the
men carrying their packages. At one point, a man
holds his cane out in front of Liam, making him
jump to avoid being struck by its tip.

They turn onto a quieter street, away from the

loud bustle. "We are nearly there," James says as they cross the street. Suddenly, a horse whinnies loudly, rising onto its hind legs as Aria and Liam stand before it. The coachman shouts at them to get out of the way, his face flushing with rage.

The three of them march away, the man's insults echoing. Suddenly, James comes to a halt and begins to rub his head. He scans the area, searching for something. "What is it?" Liam asks with a hint of relief in his voice. He's glad for an excuse to stop and catch his breath.

James begins to walk faster, peering through the windows of the houses bordering the sidewalk.

His gaze settles on a fifteen-year-old shoeshine boy.

"Hello, mate!" James says. The boy glances up from the paper he is reading with indifference. Sitting in the tall chair, his face is hidden behind a falling curtain of hair. He gives James a blank stare before asking, "What do you want?"

"I need to get to Lord Montgomery's gallery," James says. "It's an emergency!"

The boy holds out an open palm towards him. Groaning in frustration, James searches the depths of his pockets for a coin but comes up empty-handed.

Growing impatient, Aria intervenes, "Can you please tell us where Lord Montgomery's gallery is? We're in a bit of a hurry!"

The boy's voice is harsh and unwavering as he responds. "No money, no information."

Liam takes a step back in disbelief. "Are you serious? People's lives are in danger, and you don't want to help out with a simple direction?"

The boy steps toward Liam, glaring at him. "That's codswallop."

Aria and Liam grimace in confusion. James explains, "It means nonsense, rubbish! It's something you wouldn't hear in high society." The two give him a nod of thanks. Liam steps forward toward the boy and attempts to look intimidating by puffing out his chest and furrowing his brows. Aria responds to this show with an eye roll before her gaze falls upon a woman entering a building. She tugs Liam's arm, pointing excitedly towards the entrance. "Look! Baroness Orczy is right there!"

"Let's go in!" James says.

They sprint towards the door, their hearts pounding with fear and excitement. As they reach it, they pause to peer through the window, only to be met with a thick curtain blocking their view. Determined to uncover the truth, the three of them cautiously enter the deserted house. The eerie silence envelops them as they make their way through the vestibule, admiring the beautiful paintings adorning the walls. The sound of voices echoes from a distant room down the hallway.

They move forward carefully, trying not to make any noise. Aria abruptly stops as she spots the same painting that had intrigued her during her first visit to Lord Montgomery's mansion.

"Aria, come on," Liam whispers, urging her forward. Noticing her fixation, he joins her and looks at the art piece. "This painting looks familiar," he murmurs.

"You saw it in the Doyles' library," Aria replies, her voice serious.

Liam frowns. "But how can there be two identical paintings?"

"That's a good question."

"Maybe we're getting confused. We might have seen it in one of the museums we did the past two days. If I'm being honest, they all look the same!"

Their hearts race at the sudden, piercing scream. They waste no time as they rush to the end of the hallway and fling open the door, revealing a massive room decorated with large, extravagant artworks.

They halt in shock as they discover the baroness lying on the ground and Lord Montgomery hovering over her, a pistol in his grip.

His eyes widen at the sight of the three children, his voice trembling. "She... she attacked me with this gun," he stammers.

CHAPTER 24
THE IMPOSTER

Mary Louise races through the streets of London, unsure where to go. She is certain of only one thing: she must find the others. But where could they be?

After half an hour of frantic running, she decides to visit Dr. Watson's office, a location that has yet to be explored in their investigations. This is most likely where Aria, Liam, and James would go next.

She hastens to his office, her cheeks flushed and her body sweaty as she steps inside. After her initial shock, the secretary informs her that Dr. Watson isn't in and has canceled all his appointments.

As she pauses at the corner, deep in thought, her eyes land on the Scotland Yard sign across the street.

Without hesitation, she darts through the bustling crowd and bursts into the station, panting for breath. Her attention is drawn to a red-haired man conversing with the receptionist. Recognizing the curl of hair beneath his hat, she gasps—it's Mr. Parker.

Q

LORD MONTGOMERY IS IN DISBELIEF. "She tried to attack me!" he exclaims. Aria, Liam, and James watch the baroness, motionless on the floor. "I was showing her a painting when she suddenly pulled out a gun!" He gestures with the weapon, causing them to step back.

"Is she..." Liam starts, his face a mask of shock.

"No, I only hit her with the pistol after disarming her," Lord Montgomery clarifies.

"But how..." James is stunned.

"I should've seen it coming," the lord admits. "I've been receiving blackmail letters, just like Doyle. I never thought she'd be involved or wouldn't have invited her here. Now I see my mistake."

Aria frowns. "Did you know about Doyle's blackmail letters?"

Lord Montgomery approaches. "Yes, he asked

me for advice a few weeks ago. I was not their target back then, so I only advised him to ignore them. But a few days ago, I started receiving the same letters!"

"But why target you?" Liam asks.

"The adult world is complex, you see. I'm prominent in my field and know secrets that could disrupt powerful groups like the Freemasons."

"But the baroness isn't in the Freemasons," James interjects, gesturing towards her.

Lord Montgomery offers a sympathetic gaze. "I know—however, I've heard rumors about her relationship with Dr. Watson. It wouldn't be surprising if they were having an affair. Nonetheless, this is not something for children to take care of. You should return to your parents; I will call the police."

"We need to find Doyle," Aria insists.

Lord Montgomery's expression briefly flashes with anger, then returns to calm. "The police will manage it. They're excellent investigators."

Liam chuckles. "Not in our experience. We're better off searching on our own."

"You're just kids. Let the adults handle this," he says, his voice quivering.

"Lord Mont—" Aria begins, but Dr. Watson suddenly enters, silencing the room with his presence. His expression grows concerned as he glances at the lifeless baroness before turning his gaze to Aria, Liam, and James.

"What are you three doing here? This is no place for you. Leave at once," he orders, his voice echoing through the room.

Aria steps forward, but Liam grabs her arm, holding her back. "We won't leave until we find Doyle. You and your Freemasons have taken him somewhere, and now you're trying the same with Lord Montgomery! We won't let you succeed!"

Dr. Watson is taken aback. "What do you mean? He's the one who abducted Doyle!" He points an accusing finger at Lord Montgomery.

The nobleman turns to face Watson. "The gallery is closed," he says sternly.

"That's even better. As Freemasons, we hate public scenes. You're caught red-handed. The police will be here soon," Dr. Watson replies coolly.

"You're framing me for your crime. Clever, Watson, just like the character in Doyle's books," Lord Montgomery retorts.

Dr. Watson laughs scornfully. "You wish I was out of the picture. I know about your schemes. I couldn't save Doyle, but I won't let you harm the baroness." Lord Montgomery tightens his grip on the pistol. "You might take me down, but the Freemasons and justice will prevail."

"Are you seriously trying to play the victim here?" Liam asks incredulously.

Aria jumps in, "It's the classic oppressor playing the victim! You underestimated us. You blackmailed Doyle to stop him from exposing Freemason's secrets in his new book. When he resisted, you made him disappear. We know everything! We investigated!"

"And better than the police! You tried to stop us with the baroness by holding Mary Louise captive and trying to make us leave, but we won't let evil people win!" Liam says determinedly, his expression full of fury.

Dr. Watson shakes his head, his forehead furrowing in disbelief. "This is nonsense! You let your imaginations run wild, and it's gotten you nowhere. This man," he says while pointing at Lord Montgomery, "has kidnapped Doyle and is now trying to do the same with the baroness, but you stand by his side?"

"That's codswallop!" Lord Montgomery exclaims, glaring at Dr. Watson.

Aria freezes, her face's expression tightening. "Codswallop...impostor...one stone away..." she speaks in a low, murmured voice, her eyebrows knitting together. Suddenly, her face brightens as she tightens her grip on Liam's arm and hisses urgently, "He's not American!" Liam looks at her with perplexity. "Codswallop! He's from England, and I guess he's not some high society type he pretends to be. That's why the Ouija board said imposter!" she screams. She glances at Lord Montgomery, who watches her with murderous eyes.

Liam's face contorts as the solution to the mystery clicks in his mind. "Aria, remember that movie with the couple making fake paintings?"

Aria's eyes light up. "The stain on the envelope had paint on it! And his hands." She points at Lord Montgomery. "They're rough like…"

"Like someone who paints a lot!" Liam interjects, excitement growing as the pieces fall into place.

"And remember, the cook said he acted more like a British lord than an American," Aria adds, under the surprised gazes of everyone.

Dr. Watson stares in disbelief, then realizes, "You're British. Of course. How did we miss that?" He turns to Lord Montgomery, whose expression is now disdainful.

"But why go after Doyle? He's just an author," Aria asks him.

Liam interjects, "Finally, you admit it!"

Dr. Watson stares at Lord Montgomery. "He's more than that. Doyle's Sherlock Holmes has changed policing. No forensic evidence, no psychological analysis... Doyle has exposed their flaws. Soon, police will use fingerprints to analyze poisons and blood... They will have laboratories to examine all the evidence. Exactly like Sherlock Holmes! Criminals will be caught more easily. They don't like that."

"That's why he opposed Doyle's revival of Sherlock Holmes!" Liam realizes.

"And why he targeted Baroness Orczy. Doyle was her mentor; she could write similarly," Aria deduces, then turns to Watson. "That's why you asked her to disappear?" Watson nods.

"Enough!" Lord Montgomery shouts, his face red with rage. He raises his gun at Dr. Watson, who stands unflinching.

The door suddenly bursts open, drawing everyone's gaze. Chief Brown appears in the doorway with his gun drawn. "Nice timing, Chief Brown!" Dr. Watson remarks, never taking his gaze away from Montgomery's face. "Lord Montgomery, or I don't even know how to call you now, your criminal journey ends here."

Lord Montgomery smirks. "Are you sure?"

Chief Brown points his gun toward Dr. Watson, sharing a sly smile with Montgomery.

Aria, Liam, and James gasp, realizing their hopeless situation.

CHAPTER 25

NOT JUST AN AUTHOR

D r. Watson chuckles, rubbing his forehead, then looks up at Chief Brown. "I should've realized you were involved. You've been helping him all along."

"That explains the empty report," Liam says, looking at Brown, who quickly aims his gun at Liam. Dr. Watson steps in front of Aria and Liam, shielding them.

Brown laughs. "The police salary isn't great."

Aria glances between Lord Montgomery and Chief Brown. "That's why you're struggling financially!" she says to Lord Montgomery. "He's demanding more money to keep your secret."

"Money won't be a problem much longer. I have valuable paintings to sell," Montgomery replies.

"But if you duplicate paintings, you'll be caught," Liam argues.

"I won't repeat that mistake. Once you're gone, I can resume my operations."

James, silent until now, asks, "But why? Why do all this?"

"It's greed and a desire for power," Aria speaks boldly as she glares at Lord Montgomery. "You probably weren't born wealthy. Maybe you went to America seeking success. You're talented at painting, but things didn't work out. So, you turned to forging paintings, selling them as originals for profit." Lord Montgomery is speechless as Aria unfolds his life story.

Liam takes his turn. "Great job, my dear Aria! Now let me continue." He glances toward the lord with a smirk. "You scammed people in America, but they started to realize something was wrong, so you returned here. You married into high society to gain power and access to rich people. But as police methods improved, thanks to Sherlock Holmes, Chief Brown discovered your scam. You paid him off. When Doyle planned to revive his famous detective, you blackmailed him. When that failed, you kidnapped him..." Liam trails off, the rest unknown.

James gasps at his teammate. "How did you figure that out?"

"Easy," Aria replies confidently. "We used human psychology and deduction—just like Sherlock Holmes!"

Lord Montgomery marches forward, prompting everyone to step back. "Impressive theories. But it's over now," he sneers, raising his gun. An ear-splitting sound fills the room as he's about to pull the trigger. Uniformed police officers burst in, quickly disarming Chief Brown at the door. A tall man in a black suit approaches Montgomery, flanked by officers. "Mr. Montgomery, you're under arrest for fraud, impersonation, and kidnapping. Anything you say can be used against you in court."

The officers cautiously advance towards Lord Montgomery, who still clutches his pistol. "Don't move, or I'll shoot!" he threatens.

He stops short as the policemen make way for Lady Harrington to step through. Seeing his wife approach makes his heart race, the click of her heels echoing in the room. She looks more impressive than ever, standing tall and confident. She halts a short distance away, locking eyes with her husband.

"Isabella... Why are you here?" Lord Montgomery stammers, still pointing his pistol.

She laughs softly, her serious gaze making him uneasy. "You think of me as just a pretty thing without a mind, William. Like a fancy bag, you show off. But I have a brain, and I saw right through you. You shouldn't have underestimated me."

Lord Montgomery's face turns as red as a ripe tomato. "What have you done?" he blurts out, his voice shaky.

Lady Harrington can't hold back; she bursts into laughter so bright and loud that it sends a wave of surprise through the crowd. "What have I done?" she repeats, her eyes twinkling with malice. Lady Harrington bursts out laughing so intensely that a chill goes through the crowd. "Oh, William, you've got it all wrong. You are responsible for your own demise. You thought I was just another one of your helpers, but guess what? I've been watching you closely. When I found that sneaky letter you tried to send to Doyle, everything made sense. I knew my intuition about you was right."

"How dare you read my letters!" Lord Montgomery explodes.

"You're the one who told Mary Louise!" Aria points out.

"Yes, I had to tell someone."

Liam frowns. "But why not tell the police? Or Sir Doyle himself?"

"I couldn't. I didn't know why he was black-mailing Sir Doyle. And now that I do, I see you've outdone yourself, husband."

"Well, I'm cleverer than you thought."

"Not as clever as me," Lady Harrington smiles before turning to Aria and Liam. "I couldn't risk going to Doyle or the police without knowing if he had accomplices. And my caution pays off, considering what we uncover. I needed to confide in someone beyond suspicion, and who better than a child? A child's loyalty is unmatched, the purest form of trust. I bet on her taking action, hoping we could resolve the situation without the police involvement. Why? I didn't want my daughter's name tarnished or caught up in a scandal. A story like this will destroy her reputation and her chance to make a good marriage."

"Are you seriously thinking about marriage and not the innocent lives of others?" Liam intervenes, his disbelief plastered on his face. Lady Harrington fixes her gaze on him, sending a shiver down his spine.

"Because you think a woman can survive in this world without a husband? My parents sold me to this man to save their land without a care about what I wanted. Like too many other women, I wasn't seen as a person but as something to be exchanged. And now, because of the choices my husband made, my daughter and I are the ones who will suffer. We'll find doors closed to us, and faces that once smiled in our direction will look away."

Lord Montgomery laughs mockingly. "Stop whining! You nobles think you're so superior, but you're no better than anyone else!" He advances, waving his gun angrily at everyone.

The Baroness, lying unconscious behind him, slowly opens her eyes. She gazes at the situation before her, her face twisting in incomprehension. She rises from the ground, shock taking her breath away as she sees her attacker threatening others.

As she quickly assesses the situation, she seizes the perfect opportunity and strikes Montgomery with a counterfeit painting. A yelp of pain escapes him as he drops the gun, giving the police the chance to apprehend him.

Aria, Liam, and James exhale in relief as Mary Louise rushes into the room. She screams before jumping into James' arms, joyfully embracing him. "I was so worried! I went to find you when I learned my father had rejoined the Freemasons, realizing they weren't involved in the plot! But you solved it all by yourself!"

Liam smiles weakly. "Actually, Dr. Watson solved the case."

Dr. Watson clarifies, "That's not true. The evidence gathered in your investigation list in Mary Louise's room led us to Lord Montgomery. Without you, we will never have unmasked him."

"But we never completed that list..." Aria starts, confused.

"I finished it!" Mary Louise beams before turning to the men. "But how did you find it?"

"Your mother discovered it and gave it to us. You should not be mad at her. Realizing you were in danger, she pretended to play along to get you to leave. You're very determined! And we didn't know who Aria and Liam were." He smiles at them.

"And we still don't," Mr. Parker adds.

Aria and Liam exchange knowing looks, aware adults might not believe their story.

"So that's why you were spying on the Doyle house?" James questions Mr. Parker.

"Yes, we knew they were in danger but couldn't find who was behind it."

"Sorry for accusing you," Liam apologizes, making the two men chuckle.

The moment's excitement is quickly quelled when Mary Louise asks, "Where's my father? Is he dead?"

Baroness Orczy, still recovering from her ordeal, speaks up. "He's probably jailed in the cave." Everyone is taken aback but then filled with optimism when the Scotland Yard Director gives his men his order to search the area.

"He threatened to imprison me for life with Doyle. He's a bad man, but I don't think he's a killer," the baroness says.

"He went to great lengths for money…" James adds.

"Lots of people do! We've encountered many people like him on our adventures," Liam proudly says. The adults exchange curious glances at this response.

Suddenly, a man shouting Mary Louise's name appears in the doorway. At once, her heart fills with joy as she recognizes her father, who rushes to her side and embraces her.

After a heartfelt reunion, Doyle turns to Aria and Liam. "Thank you for everything. I am sorry for the misjudgment," he says. Turning to his Freemason friends, he adds, "And to you as well. I am glad to be back in the group."

Aria, blushing, suggests, "Maybe you can include our adventure in one of your stories."

"I think it's your story to write," Doyle smirks. "But first, I need a bath and to find my wife. She must be so worried." Lady Doyle appears as he speaks these words, tears of joy in her eyes. They run towards each other, their embrace leaving no doubt that love connects them. When Louisa catches sight of her daughter, she opens her arms wide. Mary Louise steps closer and wraps her arms around her mother, whispering apologies.

"I am sorry for everything, darling," Louisa says to her. "I wanted so much to keep you out of harm's way. I realize now I should not have been untruthful with you, but as a parent, I felt the need to guard you."

"It's okay, Mama."

The group falls silent as Lady Harrington approaches. "They have taken him to the police station. I guess we will be leaving London with Victoria. I want to spare her from the atrocity of the scandal." She closes her eyes for a moment to hold back a tear. "This is a goodbye, and I am truly sorry for everything."

Louisa takes her hand. "You don't need to leave. What happened is not your fault, Isabella! We will not turn our back on you."

Doyle jumps in, hopeful. "That's not going to happen,' he says. 'I've got a plan. You and Victoria can stay with us in Undershaw until things calm down. Give it a few months, and a new story will grab everyone's attention. Soon, this will all be forgotten."

Lady Harrington smiles warmly. "I'm really

thankful for your kindness," she says, then looks at Louisa. "You've got an amazing family. You're so lucky to have such a wonderful husband."

Doyle clears his throat. "I am the lucky one."

"I need to talk to Victoria before she hears about it from the news," Lady Harrington says, nodding goodbye.

Louisa looks at Aria and Liam. "I owe you both an apology for kicking you out. I hope it didn't cause too much trouble."

"Not at all. James's mother was very kind to us!" Aria says in response.

Louisa casts a glance at James. "Have we met before?"

"I deliver your milk, ma'am," he replies meekly.

"He's my friend, Mama!" Mary Louise interjects, her heart pounding. Her mother opens her mouth before Doyle interrupts, politely asking them to leave. Louisa smiles at James as she walks away with her husband.

"And don't forget my dinner party tonight," Baroness Orczy chimes in, smiling despite the day's events. "I won't let today's chaos spoil it!"

Laughter fills the air as the group heads outside. Mary Louise hangs back with Aria and Liam. "But we still haven't found who sent me the warning note!"

Both of their faces scrunch up at the same time. "Oops, we forgot to tell you!" Aria blurts out, then quickly fills Mary Louise in.

As they leave, Liam stops Aria. "I am sure Lord Montgomery had accomplices. It's impossible he managed to do this alone! We need to find out who."

"Liam, are you hooked on detective work now?" Aria teases.

"I just want to do my job right!" Liam protests.

"Your job?" Aria asks, amused, as they step out of the room. In a sudden turn of events, they are transported back to the corridor of the Sherlock Holmes Museum. Mrs. Thompson bursts out of the laboratory, her face filled with anger and disappointment. She reprimands them for ignoring her previous warnings, causing every student in the class to stare at them in shock and disapproval.

"We're sorry," Aria and Liam murmur.

Mrs. Thompson, unimpressed, assigns them a month of detention to contemplate their actions. She leaves them standing there, a bit stunned.

"Well, that's our thanks for solving a century-old mystery," Liam says, his tone dripping with sarcasm.

Aria, struck by a sudden thought, rushes back to

the room they started in. As Liam joins her, he finds her standing in front of a frame. The newspaper front page about Doyle's disappearance has been replaced with one announcing Sherlock Holmes's return.

"We got detention, but it was worth it, right?" Aria says, smiling.

Liam grins. "Definitely. And it's amazing how an author can change the world. Sherlock Holmes was revolutionary because of his unique method of solving cases. First, he just observed—no questions, no jumping to conclusions. Just by looking carefully at the scene, he could answer basic questions. Then, he'd come up with a theory, something he believed could be true, and he'd set out to prove or disprove it. After that, he'd follow every clue, ruling out the wrong paths until only the correct one remained. Imagine if Sir Arthur Conan Doyle hadn't dreamed up Holmes and his detective techniques; we might not even have forensic departments now and still deal with an unorganized police!"

Aria nods, inspired. "Exactly. And it's not just authors. You can be effective in many ways!" She turns to Liam. "You know what? I might become an author after all. I might not be the best at writing, but I have the imagination for it!"

Liam smiles proudly. "Just make sure you do an accurate portrayal of me!"

"If you want, I won't use you."

Liam frowns. "Can you really write me off?"

"Never, brother!" They both laugh, rejoining their classmates in the first forensic laboratory ever in history.

Dear Young Readers,

I hope this letter finds you well and with a keen spirit for adventure, much like my own stories. I've penned down this note to guide you through the labyrinth of fact and fiction that you've traversed in the pages of the book about me, Sir Arthur Conan Doyle.

Firstly, I must tell you about Lord Montgomery, a character brimming with intrigue and mystery. He is, I must confess, a fabrication of imagination, as is the tale of my kidnapping. I have had plenty of adventures, but never such as this.

Now, onto a matter that did indeed happen. When I decided to no longer write about Sherlock Holmes, it caused quite a storm. Many were displeased, to say the least, and made their opinions known through letters that were far from kind. Some even went to the extent of canceling their subscription to "the Stand, the magazine that published the Sherlock Holmes stories. But Holmes was an integral part of my life, so much so that he began to overshadow everything else. I wanted to spread my wings and explore other realms of writing, which led to this decision.

A fact that might surprise you is that I was indeed a spiritualist. I founded and contributed to numerous studies on the paranormal. The unseen world fascinated me greatly, and I sought to learn more about it. I was also part of the Freemasons and left before rejoining in 1902.

The love for my wife was another profound truth. I cherished her deeply and remained at her side until her untimely departure from this world due to tuberculosis.

Sherlock Holmes, a name that resonates with deduction and intellect, made his return in 1903. The world had not seen the last of him, nor he of the world. His methods, inspired by keen observation and logical deduction, influenced real-life policing and investigative techniques, laying the groundwork for modern forensic science. This legacy of Sherlock Holmes is as tangible as the streets of London.

Remember, some characters are based on real people. Beyond Mary Louise and Louisa, Baroness Emma Orczy was a crime novel author like myself, and Dr. James Watson was a friend who inspired the character Watson in the Sherlock Holmes stories.

Lastly, I want you to remember that there are many ways to make a difference in the world. It's a common misconception that only those in political jobs or royalty can effect change. Every profession, every act of creativity and kindness, has the potential to reshape our world. Remember, it is not the title that honors the person but the person that honors the title.

With warm regards and a twinkle of adventure in my eye,

Sir Arthur Conan Doyle

Hop onto our website or scan the QR code below to learn more about Sir Arthur Conan Doyle, the other characters and uncover thrilling historical facts straight from the books!

https://ariaandliam.com/blogs/aria-fun-history-class

Dear fellow adventurers,

Wowza! We're bursting with excitement as we scribble these words to thank you for joining us on this mind-blowing adventure!

Before we wrap up this wild ride, we want to shout a big THANK YOU to you, our fearless fellow adventurer. Your support, energy, and pure awesomeness have made this adventure one for the record books.

Now, as you close this book and head back to your everyday lives, remember to keep that adventurous spark alive. Let curiosity be your compass, keep exploring, and let your imaginations run wild! The world is a playground of endless wonders waiting just for YOU.

So, until we meet again, may your days be filled with endless laughter, wild adventures, and the most epic tales ever told!

Stay curious!

Cheers!

Aria   Liam

CHECK OUT ALL THE

ADVENTURES

WE'VE BEEN IN

A thrilling Egyptian adventure.

Save Caesar and face Rome's hidden challenges.

Navigate Atlantis's secrets to break a powerful curse.

Race against time to save the Incas.

Spooky thrills in Dracula's realm.

An adventure into Santa's realm to save Christmas.

A magical quest to recover Excalibur and reshape history.

A cryptic case to outsmart a mastermind and rescue Sir Arthur Conan Doyle.

www.ariaandliam.com

@ariaandliamofficial

@ariaandliam

Aria & Liam

Aria & Liam

ACKNOWLEDGMENTS

A heartfelt thank you goes out to Kay and the talented illustrators' team at Draftss, whose creativity truly brought the story to life through captivating images. I'm immensely grateful to my editors, Jane de Roussan and Alexandra, for their invaluable advice and diligent work on this book. A special expression of gratitude is owed to Stella Marvin, whose insights as a beta reader proved to be incredibly valuable.

Last but certainly not least, a big thank you to all the adventurous souls who have joined Aria and Liam on their thrilling adventure. Your support means the world.

Coline M.

ABOUT THE AUTHOR

Coline Monsarrat is a history enthusiast driven by a feverish passion for the captivating and unforgettable stories that unfold within its pages. In her series, *Aria & Liam*, she merges humor and adventure, presenting the colorful escapades of a clumsy duo navigating history and its legends. Through their journey, young readers uncover history's lessons amidst fun-filled adventures.

f facebook.com/ColineMonsarratAuthor

○ instagram.com/colinemonsarrat

Milton Keynes UK
Ingram Content Group UK Ltd.
UKHW041705210324
439830UK00004B/54